S
M

W9-BMN-919

TENDER JOURNEYS

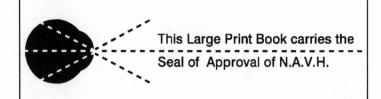

This Large Print Book carries the
Seal of Approval of N.A.V.H.

NEW MEXICO SUNRISE #3

TENDER JOURNEYS

FAITH AND LOVE HOLD
GENERATIONS TOGETHER

TRACIE PETERSON

THORNDIKE PRESS

An imprint of Thomson Gale, a part of The Thomson Corporation

Detroit • New York • San Francisco • New Haven, Conn. • Waterville, Maine • London

THOMSON
GALE
™

LIBRARY OF CONGRESS CATALOGING-IN-PUBLICATION DATA

Peterson, Tracie.
    Tender journeys : faith and love hold generations together / by Tracie Peterson.
      p. cm. — (New mexico sunrise ; no. 3) (Thorndike Press large print christian fiction)
    ISBN-13: 978-0-7862-9469-5 (lg. print : alk. paper)
    ISBN-10: 0-7862-9469-8 (lg. print : alk. paper)
    1. Large type books. I. Title. II. Series.
PS3566.E7717T46 2007
813'.54—dc22   2007002215

Published in 2007 by arrangement with Barbour Publishing, Inc.

Printed in the United States of America on permanent paper
10 9 8 7 6 5 4 3 2 1

Dedicated to my mother, Jeanine.
Her dream for me never died.

Dear Readers,

I'm happy to tell you about the re-release of eight previously published **Heartsong Presents** romances. First issued under the name Janelle Jamison, this collection launched my fiction writing ministry.

New Mexico Sunrise is book one in a two-book collection that follows the lives of the Lucas, Monroe, and Dawson families.

I hope you'll enjoy the collection in this book, as well as the one which follows in book two, New Mexico Sunset. *God bless you!*

Tracie Peterson

CHAPTER 1

1884

Jenny Oberling made her way through the rain, struggling to keep her shawl from falling into the mud as she fought against the wind and the large wicker basket she balanced on her head.

Dampness had permeated every part of her body until she could no longer control the chattering of her teeth. How good it would feel if she could make her way home into her mother's waiting arms. But Jenny's mother had been dead a little over six years, thanks to the Apaches.

There was no one, Jenny thought as she battled the storm. Because of the Indians, her family was dead and there would never again be warmth or love for Jenny Oberling.

Across town, David Monroe kicked the mud off his boots and deposited his rain-drenched coat on a peg inside the door. He was soaked from the deluge of water, which even now continued to fall.

He worked quickly to get a fire going in the small wood stove, grateful for shelter away from the damp, September air. Settling down to warm his hands, he smiled to himself. Despite the rain and mud, he was happy.

At twenty-two, the soon-to-be-pastor was eagerly anticipating his new work. He was learning to minister to the Indians of the Southwest, a mission he felt strongly God called him to.

"I see you made it without floating away," observed an older man as he entered through a door opposite the one David had used.

"Didn't think I would," David replied with a grin. "When you said it was going to rain a bit, I didn't think I had anything to worry about. You should have told me it would be in proportion to Noah and the flood."

The older man laughed heartily and set a plate of hot food in front of his apprentice. "This is what they call a gully washer. Those little gullies that crisscross the trails can quickly become raging rivers in a rain like this."

"I can believe it," David said as he dug in and ate.

"So, what do you think of our little town?"

"Well, I tell you, Ed. When I came here after weeks on the trail, I thought Santa Fe was the prettiest place I'd ever laid eyes on," David said, pausing to let his bread soak in the thick beef stew.

"And now?"

"Now," David said as he wrinkled his brow, "I'm certain of it. Of course the company I've kept has helped me fit in. But in this rain, I'm surprised the adobe doesn't melt and wash away."

Ed Clements laughingly agreed. After twelve years of being a widower, the aging pastor was enjoying David's companionship.

"Santa Fe is like a graceful, aging woman," Ed mused. "Of course, everything looks a little drab in the rain, but once the storm passes, you'll see."

"Oh, I don't need to wait," David said, thinking back on the hours he'd spent walking through the city. "The old Spanish missions are incredible, so regal and stately. Even the cemeteries are beautiful."

"It's hard to imagine them being here for centuries. The Spanish were very dedicated to the quest of winning the Indians to their faith. The missions were built to stay, and stay they have," Pastor Ed said as he reflected on the city.

"It seems to me the entire city was dedicated to mission work," David remarked. "The churches are everywhere, and those that aren't still standing have left plenty of relics behind to remind folks of their passing."

"You must understand," Ed added, "that even the city name, La Villa Real de Santa Fe de San Francisco de Asis, means the Royal City of the Holy Faith of St. Francis of Assisi. Lucky for us, they call it Santa Fe."

"I'm amazed at the people, and the devotion to their beliefs," David said as he finished his lunch. "Although I've noticed some people have more dedication to ceremony and icons than toward anything else."

"Oh, there are always some who want to be part of something simply to belong. Most people take their religion quite seriously, however. The Indians have many spirits they honor. They're often like the Greeks and Romans of Paul's day."

"How so?" David questioned.

"Well, some tribes don't have a problem in accepting yet another spirit to honor. The white man's God is powerful. They've seen many examples of white man's success and can only conclude his God must be capable of great things. Others, however, won't listen to a word you say. You present the Bible to them and it means nothing because it's a white man's book. It makes mission work here quite challenging."

"I never thought of it that way," David said as he considered the older man's words.

"When you preach before your own people, they readily accept the Bible as the Word of God. Even the hardest heart doesn't mock the Word, at least not very often. But when you sit down to speak with the Indians, it isn't just the language barrier that frustrates your efforts; it's the cultural barriers as well. You hold up the Bible and tell them it's the one truth they must accept, and they look at you like you're loco."

David nodded, "I guess that's only fair. We think them strange to worship creation rather than the Creator."

"That's right," Ed agreed. "What seems strange to us, we must turn around and see in relationship to what we preach. The Bible is simply a book of words they can't read or understand. The stories aren't part of their past, and the need for a Savior is not part of their ancestral beliefs."

"Then how do you get them to accept the need for Christ?" David asked.

"Ah ha," Ed said with a smile, "that's

13

where we must lean on God. You must never forget, David, that you work with a partner. Never, never try to rush God. He works in His time and in His way. You must live the life and learn what the Indian ways mean to them. You must understand the Indian as well as you understand yourself, in fact, even better. If you know their needs, fears, and hopes, then you can better minister to their hearts."

"Makes a heap of sense to me."

"How about some pie? Mama Rosita brought me two big apple pies," Ed announced and left the room without waiting for David's reply.

Pushing his dinner plate away, David readily accepted the offer of dessert as Ed brought two huge pieces of pie to the table.

"I'll be making some calls this afternoon," Ed said between bites. "I was wondering if you would do me a favor."

"Name it," David answered quickly. He was eager to repay the old family friend who'd opened his church and home to David's studies.

"Well," Ed began, "if you don't have too much studying to do, I'd appreciate a hand in getting some polish on the pews. I've let things go without attention for much too long. Sometimes one of the congregation offers a hand, but with roundups and harvest, people are inclined to do their own work."

"I'd be happy to help. I've nearly finished my reading. One thing about college — whether it was back home or here — professors are fond of giving you plenty to read."

Pastor Ed smiled at his young friend. "It should come as no surprise that you'll spend a good percentage of your pastoring time reading and studying. While God inspires, we can't retire! That's my motto. People think a pastor sits around waiting for a heavenly messenger to hand over a weekly sermon. It just doesn't happen that way. Oh, there are times," Ed admitted as he pushed away from the table, "it seems as if an idea comes in a flash, but in truth I have found everything in my life is God's inspiration for His service."

David listened intently. This was one of the best things about sharing a home with Ed Clements. "They don't teach you that from a text book," David laughed.

"No indeed," Ed agreed. "I'll show you where the rags and polish are and then I'd best be on my way. I told old Mrs. Putterman I'd come and visit her today, and I surely don't want to disappoint that dear saint."

David had worked on the pews for over an hour when he heard the vestibule doors open. Thinking it too early for Ed to be returning, David called out, "Hello! I'm in here."

Clasping a basket in front of her, a young woman peered through the doorway into the sanctuary. Her dark brown hair was plastered to her face and back, acknowledgment that the rain had not yet let up.

"Can I help you?" David asked as he came forward. "You must be soaked. I have a fire going in the back room. Why don't you leave your basket by the door and come warm up?"

"I . . . don't . . . want . . ." The young woman's teeth chattered so she could scarcely speak. "To be a bother," she finally managed to say.

"No bother at all," David said as he motioned her to follow. Leading the way to the back room, David pulled out a chair and set it directly in front of the wood stove.

"This ought to get you warmed up," he said with a smile and added, "I'm David Monroe, and you are?"

"Jenny," she replied. "Jenny Oberling."

16

"It's nice to meet you, Jenny. I'm new here and don't know too many people. Pastor Ed and I are good friends though. We go way back, and he's agreed to take me in and help me ease into the ministry."

"You're a pastor?" Jenny questioned doubtfully. The man before her looked too young, too handsome, and not at all like the other pastors she'd known.

As if reading her mind, David laughed. "Everybody's got to start somewhere."

Jenny smiled only for a moment. "I didn't mean anything by it," she whispered.

"I know." David wished he could put her at ease. "What brings you to the church today? Anything I might be able to help with?"

"I don't know," Jenny answered honestly. "I was on my way home, and I felt compelled to come inside. Guess it was the rain and the cold."

"You sure about that?" David questioned. Swinging a chair around backwards, he straddled it and sat down to look Jenny in the eyes. And oh, what eyes! David said nothing for a moment as he lost himself in their rich brown depths.

Jenny grew uncomfortable and lowered her face. "I'm not sure about anything. I guess that's the trouble."

"Is that why you came here?"

"I guess," Jenny said with a shrug. "I know a lot of people who put store in prayer and such. I guess I thought it might not do any harm to check it out."

"Would you like to wait for Pastor Ed, or are you comfortable enough to sit here and talk with me?"

Jenny stared openly at David for what seemed an eternity. He had beautiful blue eyes and golden blond hair that liked to fall across his face at an angle. He seemed friendly enough, kind enough, but could she explain her heart to him?

David felt nervous as he waited for her answer. It reminded him of the first time he'd asked a girl to a barn dance. She'd made him wait for an answer, too.

Jenny noticed his discomfort and took pity on him. "I guess we can talk. Only I really don't know what about. I don't know why I'm here, and I don't know what to say."

David smiled and leaned forward against the back of the chair. "We can sit here and say nothing if you prefer it that way."

Jenny removed her wet shawl and smoothed her hair away from her face. "Are you sure I'm not taking you away from something else?"

"Just polishing pews, and that can certainly wait. Why don't I get us some coffee?" David offered as he got up and took the shawl from Jenny. He draped it across another chair and took some cups from the cupboard.

"I'd like that," Jenny said, starting to relax a bit. In the back of her mind was the knowledge she should be going home, but in her heart, an interest had been sparked she'd not expected.

David left to get the coffee, and Jenny took the opportunity to study the room for a minute. The whitewashed walls were unadorned and the furniture simple, yet the room was warm and inviting.

"Here we go," David announced. He poured coffee into each of the mugs and handed one to Jenny.

Jenny took a drink, grateful for the warmth that spread through her body. "Umm, it's good," she said, warming her hands around the cup.

"Now why don't you tell me what you were doing out in this rain?" David prompted as he took his seat and unknowingly lost his heart.

CHAPTER 2

Jenny looked down at the cup, rather than face David's intense blue eyes. "I was delivering laundry. I take in washing to help pay my way."

"Pay your way?" David questioned with a frown.

"I was orphaned about six years ago. My parents were killed by the Indians in 1878."

"What happened?" David asked as though they both had all the time in the world.

Jenny's brow furrowed momentarily. "We were part of a wagon train traveling on the Santa Fe Trail. It was about this time of year — I remember because after the heat of Kansas in August, we were grateful for the cool September nights. Pa was anxious to get to Santa Fe. He'd heard stories about cheap land and glorious views. Every day he would tell us about the kind of ranch we'd have and what kind of house we'd live in. In reality, he didn't have any idea what life down here would be like."

"Sounds like a man with big dreams," David said with a grin.

"He sure was," Jenny admitted and shared David's smile. Her young heart skipped a beat at the nearness of David's broad-shouldered frame. Jenny wondered if he, too, were a man with big dreams.

"Where did the attack come?" David asked, breaking the silence.

"We were three, maybe four, days out from Santa Fe. Everyone was excited about the trip coming to an end. I remember my mother talking about what it would feel like to take a bath in a real tub again." David smiled and Jenny continued.

"I had two older brothers, and they started talking about helping Pa with the land and how they were going to find wild horses and break them to ride. Me, I just wanted the journey to be over. Day after day it was the same thing," Jenny remembered. "I was tired of sleeping under the wagon. Do you know how tedious it is to smell dirt and sage night after night?"

"Yup," David laughed, remembering his long journey to Santa Fe. "I haven't been here long enough yet to forget that."

Jenny returned the laugh. "I've been here a lot longer than you, and I still can't forget." Her voice drifted off as if she were transported back to that distant time. "I remember listening to my parents talk long into the night. It made me feel safe, knowing they were just above me. I could hear my mother's sweet voice as she'd question my pa about Santa Fe. Night after night, he'd tell her everything he'd read or heard about the territory. He loved her so much, he never tired of telling her."

"They must have loved you a great deal too," David said as he placed his coffee cup on the table. "More coffee?"

Jenny shook her head, "No thanks. I still have some left. I'm much warmer now, and I'm sure the rain has let up some. I'm sorry I've taken up so much of your time."

"You haven't done a thing I didn't invite you to do. I'd really like it if you'd tell me the rest of the story. That is, if you feel like it."

"The Apaches struck our camp at dawn," Jenny said matter-of-factly. "I remember coming fully awake out of a deep sleep and knowing something was wrong. My mother was crying, and my pa was talking in whispers to my brothers. I was made to stay with some of the other children while our parents fought for our lives."

Jenny's voice revealed the pain that held

her heart hostage. "I never saw my parents alive again. The Indians burned the wagons, stole our horses, and killed most everyone. A handful of children and old women were all that remained when the cavalry finally arrived."

"How awful for you," David sympathized, not knowing what else to say. He'd never known anyone who'd endured something as heinous as what Jenny had described. When he was taught to deal with grief, his teachers forgot to mention that pain and suffering touched the innocent lives of children, leaving wounds that seemingly never healed.

Jenny looked beyond David's face and stared blankly at the whitewashed wall behind him. She could still see the death and destruction the Apaches left in place of living, breathing souls.

David felt desperate to get Jenny's mind off the attack. "So where do you live now?" he asked.

Jenny forced herself to concentrate on David's voice. Taking a deep breath as if to cleanse the memory, she answered, "I live just down the street with Natty Morgan. She was one of the women who lived through the attack. She took me in and told me as long as I earned my keep, I could stay on."

"Earn your keep? You were a child. You're still hardly more than a child," David said and immediately regretted the words, knowing they sounded pompous.

"I'll be seventeen on New Year's Day," Jenny exclaimed angrily, "and I haven't been a child since the day of the raid."

David noted the emotion in her voice. "You must hold a great anger for Apaches."

It was a simple statement, but Jenny nearly dropped her coffee when David spoke the words. "I hate them. I hate all Indians. They are vile, hideous people who have no souls!"

A heavy silence fell between them as David silently prayed for God's direction in how to minister to the hurting girl.

"Tell me about Mrs. Morgan," David suggested, changing the subject.

"Natty?" Jenny questioned without really expecting an answer. "Natty Morgan is a hard, determined woman. She knows the price of everything and the value of nothing. As far as Natty is concerned, everything is a commodity to be bought, sold, or worked. She has her own ideas about life, and none of them are very encouraging."

"She must be hard to live with," David offered.

"Yes and no. I think the hardest thing to live with is the negative attitude. She's a pessimist by nature, always seeing the bad and expecting the worst. But as long as you do what she wants and don't cost her too much time or money, she's content to leave you be. Though," Jenny said and paused thoughtfully, "I wouldn't want to cross her. She used to run a brothel in Texas, and rumor has it she never needed a strong man to handle the customers when things got out of hand."

"I see," David said, startled by Jenny's casual reference to a house of ill-repute.

"So you do the laundry, and Mrs. Morgan does what?" David finally questioned.

"As little as possible," Jenny laughed. "I think she's used to being taken care of. But the laundry makes us good money and I don't mind."

"But what about school?" David questioned.

"School? I've had some schooling. Enough to learn to read and write. And I can do sums and figures, too. Ma used to work with me on the trail."

"Do you like to read? I have a lot of books, and you're welcome to borrow them anytime."

"I'm not sure I'd ever have time, but it's awfully kind of you to offer," Jenny replied gratefully. He barely knew her and yet he treated her as though she were some long lost friend.

"Do you go to church?" David questioned, wondering if he could interest Jenny in coming to hear him speak on Sunday.

"No. Natty's always seen it as a waste of time. She sleeps through the morning while I work. As much as Natty hates working with dirty clothes, I never have to worry about her hanging around me much, so it's kind of peaceful. Besides, it gives me time to think."

"Think about what?" David asked gently. Jenny seemed so fragile, and David was afraid the wrong question might cause her to bolt and run.

"I think mostly about my parents and my brothers," Jenny added.

"You must miss them a lot."

Jenny nodded and took a sip of the coffee. "It used to be I'd be doing something and I was certain I heard my mother calling me. I'd get up and start to go to her, then remember she was gone." The sadness in her voice made her sound years younger.

"Sometimes I remember our last morning. I can smell the smoke and hear the screaming. Almost every night it's the same thing."

"Nightmares?" David questioned.

"Uh huh." Jenny nodded. Thunder cracked outside and she shuddered.

"You're safe here," David said softly. He longed to put a supportive arm around the girl and drive away her fears.

Jenny gave him a sad smile. "Maybe so, but I can't stay here forever."

"You can have safety and peace no matter where you go," David said determined to share the way of salvation with Jenny. "God's peace is something nobody can take from you. It's the kind of security you can count on no matter where you live or go."

"My mother believed in God. She was a Christian and read the Bible to us every night," Jenny whispered. She finished the coffee and put the cup on the table. "I really should go."

"Why?"

"Natty will be expecting me, and soon it'll be time to get supper on." Jenny realized her words sounded like an excuse.

"Will you come back, maybe even come for church on Sunday?" David asked softly as he reached out and put his hand over Jenny's. "I'd like to be your friend and maybe introduce you to a friend of mine."

"I'll think about it," she said and pulled her hand away. Getting to her feet, Jenny retrieved her shawl and allowed David to help her with it.

"You're welcome to stop by here any time you like," David said as he opened the back door. "In fact, I'd like it very much if you would. I'd like to get to know the city better, and since you've been here five years, maybe you could show me around."

"Maybe," Jenny whispered. The rain had abated, but the sky still looked heavy and dark with low hanging clouds. "I'd best go before it starts in again," she said as she hurried through the door.

As Jenny made her way down the street, she couldn't stop thinking about David Monroe. Something about him had seemed so different, so kind. He seemed to genuinely care about her, and that was something Jenny hadn't enjoyed since the death of her parents.

He wanted her to come back on Sunday. Jenny wondered if he'd be giving the sermon. As she entered Natty's house, Jenny was caught up in dreams of sitting in the congregation, listening to David.

She was just hanging her shawl up when Natty's grating voice sounded from the front room. "Where have you been?"

Jenny went to a drawer and took out a brush. "I was delivering clothes."

Natty came through the doorway, fussing

with the button on her well-worn black skirt. "You shouldn't have taken so long. Just look at yourself."

Jenny glanced down at her wet clothes and then looked up at the gray-haired woman. Natty was biting her lower lip in concentration, struggling to secure the button at the waist of her skirt.

"Let me help," Jenny offered. Natty didn't argue as Jenny pushed her pudgy hands aside and took hold of the skirt.

"You'll have to suck in," Jenny said and pulled the skirt together. "There, it's buttoned."

"Well, it's about time. Look, I'm going out, so you needn't fix supper and waste heating the stove. There are biscuits left over from breakfast, and I'm sure you can make a meal on them," Natty said and pulled on a waist jacket. "I won't be back until late."

Jenny waited until Natty was gone to heave a sigh and sit down. No doubt Natty was headed out to one of the gambling houses and wouldn't be back until the wee hours of the morning.

It was of little concern to Jenny. Her mind was still back at the church, fixed fast on David Monroe.

CHAPTER 3

When Sunday arrived, Jenny managed to sneak out of the house long enough to slip into the back pew of the Methodist Church. She kept her head covered and tried to stay hidden behind a stout man.

David took his place in the pulpit and immediately noticed the dark-haired girl who tried so hard to hide from him. He couldn't suppress a grin as he welcomed those who were regulars as well as those who were visiting for the first time.

Jenny tried not to be pleased, knowing he was referring to her perhaps more than anyone else. But in truth, it made her feel warm and happy to know he cared enough to notice her presence.

The time passed quickly, and Jenny listened intently as David spoke of God's love for the world — love that Jesus had demonstrated when He died on the cross to pay the penalty for the world's sins. Jenny felt a bit uncomfortable when David began to speak about forgiveness. How could God forgive anyone for taking the life of His Son? It would be no different than people expecting Jenny to forgive the Indians for killing her family.

David took his Bible and stepped down from the pulpit. He moved toward the first row of pews and stopped.

" 'I am the good shepherd: the good shepherd giveth his life for the sheep,' " he read from John 10:11. "The world didn't take anything from Jesus. He gave it all. He gave His life and love so you and I might live forever in forgiveness and reconciliation with our heavenly Father."

A few people in the crowd murmured "Amen," and Jenny wondered at their enthusiasm. The congregation seemed to be in perfect agreement with David's words.

To emphasize his meaning, David read more from John 10 and concluded with verses 17–18: " 'Therefore doth my Father love me, because I lay down my life, that I might take it again. No man taketh it from me, but I lay it down of myself. I have power to lay it down, and I have power to take it again. This commandment have I received of my Father.' "

Jenny couldn't take in the meaning of the

words, but she thrilled to David's rich, confident voice. When David concluded the service and asked everyone to bow their heads for the benediction, she quietly slipped out the vestibule door and hurried home. Feeling confused about David and his words, she was too nervous to face him.

Throughout the next week, Jenny worked hard to forget her feelings for David. As she scrubbed clothes at the washboard, she could almost see his sweet smile in the soapsuds. Hanging the laundry on long lines in back of the house, Jenny hummed the melody of the song they'd sung at church Sunday. She couldn't remember the words, except for the line about Jesus paying for her sins. She mingled this with her thoughts of David and a Savior's love for his people.

When Friday arrived, Jenny realized she could no longer put aside her thoughts of David and decided to go for a visit. By the time she had carefully finished ironing the last of the laundry and placed it in a huge basket, Natty was still sleeping off the night before.

Jenny briefly examined her appearance in a small mirror. She wished she looked older. Jenny studied the red gingham dress she wore and noted with satisfaction that it made her look more mature. Her brown hair was tied back at the neck and fell long and straight to her hips. She whirled around and watched as the skirt of the gown fell perfectly into place.

Jenny smoothed the eyelet lace that trimmed the square-necked bodice and pinched her cheeks even though they needed little help to be rosy. She then pulled on her wrap, secured the basket on her head, and went on her way to make the deliveries.

So excited was Jenny about the prospect of seeing David, she could scarcely remember where each bundle of clothes belonged. She hurried through town, barely pausing to say hello to the people she passed. She avoided the Indians who had gathered to trade their wares. It didn't matter they were Pueblos, known for being peaceful and friendly. They were Indians.

When she'd delivered the final bundle of shirts to Father Martinez at one of the missions, Jenny nearly ran to the Methodist Church.

David had questioned Pastor Ed about Jenny Oberling. Ed knew a little about the girl and had utilized her laundering services when he could spare the money for someone else to wash his clothes.

"She lives just down the street. I'm not

sure which house it is, but it shouldn't be hard to find. Why don't you try to find her?" Ed asked as he helped David finish putting away the breakfast dishes.

"I'd like to try," David said as he considered the possibility. "I know she needs a friend. It doesn't sound like she has any real companionship."

"No, I suppose not," Pastor Ed agreed. "The woman she lives with has a less-than-sterling reputation. Natty Morgan has a flare for the wilder side of life. I've spoken with the woman on several occasions and always met with a stone wall when it comes to church and Christianity."

"Do you suppose she would forbid Jenny from coming to church on a regular basis?" David questioned as he replaced the dishtowel on a peg.

"Nothing would surprise me," Ed replied. "Perhaps there is a way to get on Mrs. Morgan's good side, but I'm not familiar enough with the situation to know how."

David nodded. Just then a light knock at the back door caught both men's attention. David opened the door and couldn't hide his pleasure.

"Jenny!" he exclaimed. "We were just talking about you."

"About me?" Jenny questioned as she set

her basket on the ground beside the door and let her shawl fall away from her face and onto her shoulders. "Why?"

"I was just explaining to Pastor Ed that I wondered if I would see you again. You didn't tell me where you lived, so I couldn't stop by to invite you to join us for Sunday services," David replied, uncertain what else to say.

He didn't feel comfortable enough to tell Jenny it was really his concern for her well-being that made him want to call. Then again, David wasn't sure it was only Jenny's well-being that drew him to her.

"Please come in and sit down," Ed said as he came forward and offered Jenny his arm. "You're out awfully early today. Have you been making your laundry rounds?"

"Why, yes," Jenny said sweetly as she allowed Ed to offer her a chair. "Pastor Monroe —"

"Call me David," he interjected.

Jenny raised her liquid brown eyes to his and felt her heart beat faster. "David," she spoke softly, "asked me to show him around the city. I thought if he had time we might walk this morning."

David glanced briefly at Ed before accepting Jenny's invitation. "I'd be happy to."

"Good," Jenny said feeling a bit awkward.

"You know, Jenny," Ed began, "we have a gathering for our local youth. You might enjoy coming and meeting some people your own age. They meet here at the church on Sunday evenings. Sometimes they have outings and sometimes they just get together to study God's Word."

"I'll think about it," Jenny replied and lowered her gaze. "I'm not sure it would be all that easy to get out Sunday evenings. Natty usually has friends over and often needs me to put together refreshments."

"Don't feel pressured, Child. I just wanted you to know you're more than welcome."

"Thank you," Jenny said and raised her eyes only enough to meet David's.

"Well, if you're ready," David said with a smile, "I'll put on my coat and take you up on your offer."

First, Jenny led David to the city's adobe square, pointing out local oddities and points of interest. The day had warmed, and the cloudless sky was an intense blue. David listened to Jenny speak of the rich Spanish history of Santa Fe, noting she avoided discussing the Indian population.

He was sorry when Jenny led the way back to the church with the announcement she was needed at home.

"Will you come for the service on Sunday?

I'm not speaking that day, but Pastor Ed does a wonderful job and I know you'd like him."

"I'm not sure," Jenny said nervously. How could she explain to David that the Christian faith confused her? She didn't like confronting her anger and her past, and Christianity demanded she do both.

"I hope you can. Especially on Sunday evening. There are quite a few people your own age," David said. Jenny turned quickly to pick up her basket, hoping to hide her disappointment in David's reference to her youth.

"I'll think about it," she murmured. Securing her basket atop her head, Jenny made her way down the walkway.

"Well, think real hard about it," David good-naturedly called out to Jenny's retreating form.

Jenny didn't make the services on Sunday morning or Sunday evening. Natty Morgan was in a fierce mood about the money she'd lost during one of her gambling parties. Jenny knew better than to cross her, and when Natty announced she was throwing a card party on Sunday night, Jenny didn't argue.

As Jenny prepared the refreshments, anger surged within her. She didn't know which infuriated her more: the thought of not getting to see David at the service or the fact that he looked upon her as a child.

Jenny finished spooning jam into the tarts she'd baked earlier and set the buffet for Natty's friends. Everything was in place, so Jenny made herself scarce as Natty's boisterous guests began arriving.

Slipping out the back door, Jenny took a seat in their small courtyard. The night sky was filled with stars, and a huge harvest moon rose just over the horizon.

Inside the house, Jenny could hear the raucous laughter of Natty's drinking friends. How she hated her life with the vulgar woman. Jenny relaxed against the cold iron of the chair and sighed.

She tried to imagine the gathering at the Methodist Church. What would it be like to mingle among people her own age, as David had called them? Long into the night, Jenny sat and dreamed about the church group and David Monroe.

The next morning, scarcely an hour after Jenny had started her morning tasks, she was surprised by a knock on her door.

"Good morning, David," Jenny replied shyly. "What brings you here?"

"I wondered if you would have time to walk with me this morning? I know you have your chores and all, but I wondered if you could spare a few moments."

"I suppose I could," Jenny said as she went to the peg where her shawl was hanging. "Only I can't stay away too long."

"That's fine," David replied with a grin. He held the door open for Jenny and offered his arm to her as he walked beside her.

Jenny hesitated for a moment. She longed to pretend he could see her for the mature young woman she was and not the child that sixteen conjured in his mind. If only she could make him aware of her maturity. Shyly, she accepted his arm and cherished every moment as he led her down the street.

David and Jenny walked down to the river, and when David suggested they sit and talk, Jenny eagerly agreed. Perhaps now she could prove herself to be older and wiser than David Monroe realized.

"It's really beautiful down here," David said as he took a seat on the ground beside Jenny. "I happened down here the first day I was in town. I've been coming back whenever time allows."

"It is nice," Jenny agreed and spread her calico skirt out in an attractive manner.

"I missed seeing you yesterday," David

began, "and I couldn't get you out of my mind."

Jenny's heart gave a leap. "You couldn't?" she whispered.

"Truth is, since the first day you walked into the church looking like a drowned rat, I haven't been able to put you far from my thoughts." David said with a smile.

"Drowned rat, eh?" Jenny questioned, cocking her head to one side.

David's smile broadened. "But a very fetching drowned rat." Jenny blushed and said nothing. "Look, Jenny," David continued, "I've been very worried about you for reasons I can't explain. I guess the Lord has laid a burden of concern on my heart for you."

"I don't understand," Jenny replied. "Why would God want you to worry about me?"

"He cares for you, Jenny," David stated evenly. "He wants the best for you, and perhaps, this is His way of getting you to see that."

"I haven't had much religion in my life since the Indians killed my family. I'm not sure I can trust enough to believe all those things you say about God," Jenny admitted.

"Trust is a big part of Christian faith. People are always wanting answers for the things that happen in their lives. Something bad takes place and people want to receive an immediate answer from the Almighty for the wherefores and whys."

"Trust is hard when you've got nothing to base it on," Jenny said as she picked at the scraggly yellow grass.

"God's love is the best foundation you could ever have. Trust matures and grows with each day that you give yourself over to Him. God loves all His children and wants them to know and believe in His love."

"Even the Indians?" Jenny questioned and eyed David's face.

David's expression softened. "Even the Indians, Jenny. You can't condemn an entire race of people for the actions of a few. A renegade band of Apaches attacked your wagon train and killed your loved ones — not all Indian nations, not even the entire Apache tribe. Jenny, just as there are evil people among the whites, there is evil among other races as well."

"I've never thought of it that way," Jenny had to admit. "I've always thought all Indians were alike."

"Up in the town of Cimarron, some pretty tough characters caused a lot of trouble. Would it be fair if the rest of the nation judged the people of the New Mexico Territory by those few troubled souls in Cimarron?"

"No, I suppose it wouldn't."

"Jenny, I know you're hurting and I know your loss is great. But you've grieved your loss for six years and held a consuming bitterness for just as long. You'll never be happy or at peace until you let go of that bitterness. And Jenny," David paused, "I think the reason you came into the church that first day was because you're seeking some peace of mind. Isn't that true?"

Jenny looked out across the valley. David's words had hit a nerve. How could he so easily identify her heart's deepest secrets? Finally, she spoke.

"I would like to sleep without the nightmares. Just once, I'd like to go to bed and not fear falling asleep."

"Jesus can give you that kind of peace, Jenny, but you must let go of your anger. I know it won't be easy, but I'll help you any way I can, and God will give you the strength you need to conquer your fears."

"He can't give me back my family, though," Jenny said sadly.

"But your family belonged to God," David offered. "You said your mother was a Christian."

"Oh, my pa and brothers were too," Jenny

said with a glimmer of hope in her voice.

"Then you'll see them again in heaven. Didn't anyone ever tell you one day we'll all be reunited with our loved ones in heaven? If you belong to God, you're His on earth and in heaven. In John 11:25–26, Jesus said, 'I am the resurrection, and the life: he that believeth in me, though he were dead, yet shall he live: And whosoever liveth and believeth in me shall never die. Believest thou this?' "

"Do you believe it?" Jenny asked, feeling completely at ease with David's tender approach. "Do you believe God can take away the hurt?"

"I know He can, Jenny. I believe in salvation through Jesus Christ with all my heart. It's the reason I became a minister. I wanted very much to share the Gospel with a hurting world."

"I have to admit, nothing else has worked. I want very much to get on with my life and not always be concentrating on the pain and memories of what used to be."

David smiled and reached out to take hold of Jenny's hand. "I knew you felt this way. I felt so strongly that God wanted me to share this with you."

"What do I do now?" Jenny questioned.

"Well," David said with a smile, "further

in the book of John, Jesus is preparing to raise a dear friend of his from the dead. Jesus went to the tomb and told the people there, 'Take ye away the stone.' Jenny you need to take away the stone. You need to forgive what happened to your family and allow God to deal with the people involved."

"It won't be easy," Jenny said, tears sliding down her cheeks.

"No, not in your own power but in God's unlimited power, you have all the help you'll need."

"I want God to take away my stone. I want to be free once and for all, but I need time to think about this."

David let go of Jenny's hand and reached out to wipe a tear from her face. "Then we'll tell God all about it and trust Him to minister to your heart."

Chapter 4

David began to appear on Jenny's doorstep on a regular basis, and to Jenny's relief he never again mentioned her need of people her own age.

Most mornings they would venture around the city of Santa Fe. Jenny would point out different buildings and explain all she'd learned during her six-year stay in the city. The city was much bigger than David had anticipated, and with the expanded population came a bigger need for God.

One morning, Jenny took David to the Mission of San Miguel on the east side of the city.

"This mission is nearly three hundred years old," she explained as she paused for David to study the building. The first level held a second, smaller floor and on top of that was yet another smaller level. The pattern was repeated twice and gave the small mission a tower. Behind the first and second stories, the building spread out to form the remainder of the chapel.

"It's hard to imagine anything being here that long," David said as he considered the adobe and stone frame.

"It's thought to be the oldest mission in the United States," Jenny stated, "although much of the original mission was destroyed during the Pueblo Revolt. The Spanish rebuilt it in 1710."

"Ed told me the Pueblo had tired of Spanish domination, especially where their religious practices were concerned," David said and continued to study the structure. He felt awed by being able to touch history in a way few people would ever enjoy.

"Yes," Jenny said as she remembered the things she'd been told by others. "The Spanish, primarily the church leaders, were so concerned about the welfare of the people that some of the Indians were hanged as witches. Eventually, the Pueblos decided enough was enough. They held the entire countryside captive and killed everyone that moved along the way."

"I can't imagine the Indians being able to drive the mighty Spanish from this area," David said absentmindedly.

"The 'mighty Spanish,' as you call them, were forced to take refuge behind protective walls. The Indians were slaughtering every-thing in sight and were unwilling to settle for anything short of the complete with-drawal of the Spanish." Animosity colored Jenny's voice, and David decided to drop the issue.

They walked in silence as Jenny led David back to the plaza at the center of town. They paused to sit on a bench near the gazebo that stood at the center of the plaza.

"I'm intrigued by that building over there. I've heard it called by many names," David said as he tried to reestablish conversation.

"I suppose it usually goes by the name of Casas Reales. It means 'royal houses' in Spanish," Jenny replied. "I've heard it called the Adobe Place and El Palacio. Some descendants of the nobility still call it the Palacio Real or 'royal palace.' The Spanish king directed his people to build it as hous-ing for his appointed governors. This is where the Spanish took refuge during the Pueblo Revolt."

"I had no idea it was that old."

"It's thought to have been built around 1609, some seventy-one years before the revolt," Jenny offered.

"You've certainly learned a great deal about the city," David complimented.

Jenny smiled and pulled her shawl close.

47

A breeze coming down from the mountains was chilling her. David immediately noticed and suggested they make their way back to her house.

"You haven't mentioned Mrs. Morgan lately," David said as he took hold of Jenny's arm and helped her across the street.

"Not much to mention. Natty sleeps late most mornings and doesn't know whether or not I'm in the house. I don't see it as her concern anyway. I'm nearly grown and have to start thinking about what I'm going to do with the rest of my life. I can't stay with her much longer."

"I'm surprised you've stayed this long. The woman obviously depends upon you for her living."

"Not really," Jenny said with a shrug. "She's a pretty fair gambler. Most of her money for gambling and drinking comes from her own sources. My earnings keep food in the house and pay the rent. I figure I can do that on my own just as easily as I can living with Natty. In fact, I think it would be a whole lot easier."

"No doubt," David agreed. "But wouldn't it be a bit, well, a bit risqué? I mean, a young single woman living alone in the city doesn't seem fitting."

Jenny laughed. "Apparently, Pastor Ed

hasn't told you much about the uninhibited lifestyle of many in this city. Many of the married men not only keep mistresses, but their wives have, well," Jenny paused, blushing slightly, "shall we say, friends of their own."

"I had no idea," David admitted. "Do Mrs. Morgan's friends ever, uh . . ." David hesitated. "Do they ever bother you?"

Jenny's flushed face darkened. "She has some friends who make me quite uncomfortable. Mostly it's just the way they look at me. No one has ever touched me or caused me any grief, if that's what you mean. Why do you ask?"

David stopped as they reached Jenny's house. He took Jenny's hands in his and tried to find the words to explain his apprehension. "You're a beautiful young woman and it concerns me you're subjected to such a vile lifestyle. Please be careful."

David's worried expression touched Jenny's heart. Perhaps he did care for her, at least a little. "I will be," Jenny whispered and grew uncomfortable in the silence that fell between them.

"Will you have time to walk tomorrow?" David asked as he dropped his hands.

Jenny crossed her arms protectively against her body and raised her brown eyes to meet

David's stare. "I should," she replied shyly. It felt so wonderful to have David's companionship, and Jenny was reluctant to enjoy it for fear it would be snatched from her.

"Good," David said with a smile. "There's somebody I want to introduce you to. I'll come by around eight." Jenny nodded and watched for several minutes as David disappeared down the street.

She carried the warmth of David's smile with her as she went up the stone walkway, unmindful of the woman who watched her from the house.

"So that's the way it is," Natty Morgan muttered. Not wanting Jenny to find her, Natty quickly returned to her bedroom and plotted how she would handle this unwelcome change.

The following morning at exactly eight o'clock, Jenny answered the door to find David decked out in his best suit. "Oh my," Jenny said with a frown as she glanced down at her simple, pale blue, cotton gown. "I didn't expect to dress up."

"No need for you to," David said with a grin. "You always look perfect."

Jenny lowered her face but smiled at the compliment. It was becoming clear to her that David shared her deep feelings for their relationship.

"Are you ready?" David asked.

"Yes," Jenny said as she took her heavy wool shawl to ward off the morning chill.

She closed the door quietly behind her and took David's arm as he led the way down the street.

Natty Morgan slipped quietly from her bedroom and watched the young couple move down the road toward Washington Avenue. Why hadn't she realized Jenny was nearly a grown woman?

The robust woman pulled on a silk wrapper and poured herself a cup of the coffee Jenny had kept warming on the stove. How old was the child anyway? Sixteen? Seventeen? Certainly marriageable age, and if that were to happen, what would become of Natty's lifestyle? She depended on the child to wait on her and to keep their meager home together. Natty contemplated the situation for a long time before taking herself back to bed.

David led the way to the Exchange Hotel. "We're supposed to wait here," he said as he turned to Jenny. Her questioning face betrayed her concern. David's brow furrowed momentarily, then it dawned on him that leading Jenny to the Exchange Hotel was most inappropriate.

"I'm sorry, Jenny. I never thought of how

this might look to you or anyone else. Why don't I take you across the street to the park and let you wait there? I'll come back here and," David's words were interrupted by a rousing greeting from another huge, blond man.

"David!" The man rushed through the doors of the Exchange Hotel and crushed David with a bear hug. Jenny watched them silently as did a young, blond woman who was standing behind the stranger.

"Daniel, I'm so glad you're finally here. I brought someone for you to meet," David said as he reached back and pulled Jenny to stand beside him. "This is Jenny Oberling, my best friend in Santa Fe. Jenny, this is my older brother, Dr. Daniel Monroe. He's come to answer an advertisement. Seems folks up north of Santa Fe want a doctor."

"Dr. Monroe," Jenny said as she extended her small hand and found it engulfed in Daniel's large, well-manicured one.

"It's nice to meet you, Jenny. And," Daniel said as he pulled the blond woman from behind him, "this is my wife, Katie."

"Wife?" David said in shocked surprised. "You never said anything about a wife in your letter. When did you get married?"

"David," Jenny found herself admonishing the young pastor, "don't be rude. It's very nice to meet you, Katie," she added as she took Katie's hand. "Even nicer still to have someone who's near my own age. At least David keeps telling me I need to circulate among that crowd."

Daniel laughed out loud at David's stunned expression. "I've never seen anybody able to render him speechless. It's indeed a pleasure to meet you, Miss Oberling."

"Yes," Katie agreed and gave Jenny's hand a squeeze. "It's very nice to meet you."

Jenny suddenly grew embarrassed at her bold words, but before she could say anything further, David drew their attention to Katie's condition. "Why, Daniel, you've not only married a beautiful woman, but if I'm not mistaken, she's going to make me an uncle in a very short time."

"That was my prognosis," Daniel said with a smile. Katie blushed, and Jenny noticed her well-rounded stomach as David continued to pat his brother on the back.

"How wonderful," Jenny said and David agreed.

David glanced at the street clock. "Have you had breakfast yet?"

Daniel and Katie nodded. "The long trip exhausted us both so much we fell into bed without a bite of supper," Daniel explained.

"This morning we ate like ranch hands."

Katie laughed. "That's for sure. I don't think half of this is as much baby as it is fried eggs and ham," she said, patting her stomach.

"Well then," David offered, "perhaps a walk. I've the best tour guide in all Santa Fe." They all glanced at Jenny who felt her face grow hot under the startling blue eyes of the Monroe brothers.

"I'd love to see more of the city," Katie said, breaking the silence. "I've only seen what little the street lamps afforded me last night."

"I'd be happy to show it to you." Jenny said as she turned to David. "Where should we start?"

The rest of the morning was spent in nonstop chatter about the city and the old relics and buildings that gracefully lined its streets. When Jenny suddenly realized it was nearly noon, she stopped in her tracks with a stricken look.

"What is it, Jenny?" David asked, concerned she'd taken ill.

"I forgot about Natty," Jenny admitted. "She'll be up by now and wondering where I am. There will be a price to pay for this splendid morning."

"I'll take you home right now," David said

as he turned to speak with Daniel.

"No," Jenny insisted. "Natty had better not see you coming down the street with me. It would be best if I go ahead alone. Dr. Monroe, Mrs. Monroe, it was a pleasure to meet you. I hope we can spend more time together."

"Only if you call us Daniel and Katie," David's brother said with genuine affection.

"Yes, please," Katie said as she placed her hand upon Jenny's arm. "I'd like for us to be friends."

Jenny forgot her lonely, empty life and basked in the warmth of her newfound friendships. David shook his head in wonder. Could she really be the same scared and angry young woman who had burst into his life only weeks before?

Jenny hurried through the streets of Santa Fe and found Natty Morgan angrily pacing the floor.

"Where've you been?" Natty growled between clenched teeth. "The stove's cold, the coffee's thick as mud, and I haven't had as much as a biscuit to eat."

"Sorry," Jenny said and offered no other explanation. She quickly got a fire going in the stove and threw out the remains of the morning's coffee. "What would you like to eat?"

"I want eggs, toast, and potatoes," Natty said as she took a chair at the kitchen table. "And throw a steak on. I feel as though I could eat a horse."

Jenny went to the larder for the meat and eggs. Satisfied the stove was heating to a proper temperature, Jenny sliced up potatoes and ham and joined the older woman. Startled to discover she was whispering a silent blessing on the meal, Jenny smiled at David's influence in her life.

"I suppose that lovesick expression is for the young man I saw you with this morning," Natty said between stuffing huge forkfuls of food into her mouth.

Jenny's heart sank. Natty knew about David. Working to ease Natty's mind from concern, Jenny didn't deny her statement. "That 'young man' as you call him, is Pastor David Monroe. He's a new minister here working with Pastor Clements at the Methodist Church. He asked me to accompany him this morning and help his brother and sister-in-law learn their way around the city. His brother is a doctor and his sister-in-law is expecting a baby soon."

"I see," Natty replied, somewhat surprised at the detail Jenny gave. It only made her more curious, knowing Jenny was never one to volunteer information.

Jenny picked at the food on her plate, wondering how she was going to get Natty off the subject of her friendship with David.

"How did you meet this Pastor Monroe?" Natty questioned. She watched Jenny intently for any signs of discomfort.

Jenny, who'd long ago learned how to play Natty's moods and tirades, shrugged her shoulders. "I think I met him when I was delivering clothes one day." She tried to sound disinterested, wondering just how much Natty had surmised.

"Seems to me," Natty said as she pushed away from the table and tried to wipe egg yolk from her blouse, "you have a great deal more interest in this Pastor Monroe than in just being his guide around Santa Fe."

"He's very kind, and I enjoy listening to him talk about the cities back east," Jenny said, grateful she didn't have to lie. "I haven't had a chance to talk about things like that since the raid."

Natty always steered away from any reference to the Apache raid, but today she wasn't giving an inch. "What age were you when those Injuns attacked? Better yet, how old are you now, Jenny?"

Jenny nearly dropped her fork in surprise. "How old am I? I'm sixteen, nearly seventeen. You should know that Natty. My birthday's New Year's Day."

"Seventeen? Hmm," Natty said with a strange look on her face. "Seems to me most girls your age are married."

"Seems to me, most girls don't have the responsibilities I have," Jenny said sarcastically. She'd always managed to stand her ground with Natty.

"You think you've got it real bad, don't you?" Natty questioned as she picked at her teeth with the end of her knife. "Where would you have been if I hadn't taken you in? I gave you a roof over your head and food in your belly. I could have left you on the plains to be picked up by the next passing band of Apaches."

Jenny grimaced and Natty knew her words had hit home. One thing Natty knew full well was Jenny Oberling's hatred of Indians.

"A body would think a little more gratitude would be in order," Natty said in a tone of voice that let Jenny know she'd lost the argument.

"I am grateful, Natty," Jenny said as she got up and started clearing the table. "You know I am. We've never had to play games before, so why now? Why not just say what's on your mind."

Natty leaned back and smiled. "I've a mind to find you a husband. A rich one who's willing to pay a high price for a young, unspoiled white woman."

Jenny shuddered at the thought but said nothing. Perhaps if she appeared unconcerned, Natty would drop the idea. Perhaps Natty would go on gambling and drinking and forget Jenny had somehow threatened her security. Perhaps, but not likely.

Jenny went to the well and brought up a bucket of water for washing the dishes. She understood too well Natty had found a new game to play. This time, Jenny's life would be staked.

CHAPTER 5

With Daniel and Katie in Santa Fe, David had less time to visit Jenny. He'd tried to locate her on her laundry rounds, but to no avail.

He busied himself with his studies and spent more time with Pastor Ed, learning the basics about life in the Indian villages. But no matter how hard he tried, David couldn't stop thinking about Jenny and how good it felt to be in her company.

David stood shaving one morning, staring at his reflection in the small mirror that hung over the washbasin. He remembered the way Jenny had chided him when he'd met Katie. Many men might have found that moment annoying, but David remembered it with fondness because it spoke of the familiarity between him and Jenny. She would never have been comfortable enough to speak her mind had she not felt a closeness to him — of that he was certain.

He finished shaving, had his devotions, and ate breakfast all before the clock in the town square chimed seven. With the morning stretching before him, David decided to walk by Jenny's in hopes of catching her at home.

Donning his coat and hat, David was just about to step out the door, when Daniel appeared on the walkway. "I'm glad I caught you. Can you spare me some time this morning?"

"I guess so," David said and tried not to sound disappointed. "What'd you have in mind?"

"I'm supposed to meet up with the man who placed the ad for a doctor. I got a note from him last night that he'd come in with the cattle drive from up north. I'm supposed to meet him at eight o'clock."

"Who is he?" David questioned as he joined Daniel on the walk.

"Jason Intissar. He owns a ranch north of Santa Fe. In fact, several days north of Santa Fe. He's up in the mountains, has a huge valley spread as I hear tell."

"I've heard of the Intissar ranch. Isn't it called Piñon Canyon?" David asked.

"That's right," Daniel answered and gave David a hearty pat on the back. "You don't know how good it is to see you again. I thought a lot about you while I was doing my residency in Kansas City. I kept wondering if you were eating right and how school was going. I didn't even know you'd left the seminary in Iowa until Ma wrote and told me."

"Sorry," David apologized. "I kept meaning to write, but I had so much work to do."

"You don't need to tell me," Daniel said with a smile. "I've been negligent enough for both of us. You didn't know about Katie, after all."

"She's really nice, Daniel. I'm glad you found someone to love. I always prayed you would."

"You must have put just the right words into those prayers, 'cause Katie is everything a man could want. Do you know, she even wants to be my nurse when I get my practice set up?"

"It doesn't surprise me. She's pretty young, though, isn't she?" David dared the question.

Daniel frowned a bit, "Well, that's another story. I thought she was older. She lied to me about her age. Once we were married, I found out she was only sixteen, and well, the baby was already on the way. But I have to admit, her age has nothing to do with her maturity."

"I guess I can relate to that," David agreed.

"Yeah, I suppose you can. Just how old is that Jenny of yours?"

"What makes you think she's mine?" David asked with a laugh, but in truth he wondered if Daniel had picked up on something he'd missed.

"Just the way she looks at you says it all," Daniel grinned. "Katie was the same way — still is — and it never fails to make this old heart pound a little faster."

David laughed out loud.

"Well, here we are," Daniel added as they paused outside La Bonita Café. "We made arrangements to meet here."

Daniel and David were seated, and although David had eaten breakfast, he agreed to a cup of strong coffee. Daniel had just received his food when an older man and his companion approached the table.

"Are either of you gentlemen Dr. Daniel Monroe?" the older man questioned.

"I am," Daniel said, extending his hand as both he and David got to their feet.

"I'm Jason Intissar," the gray-haired man said with a smile, "and this is Garrett Lucas. He's like a son to me and assists me in most every matter on my ranch."

"It's nice to meet you both," Daniel said

as he shook hands with the men. Garrett Lucas, he noticed, hardly looked much older than his Katie. "This is my brother, Pastor David Monroe," Daniel said as he turned to David.

David took hold of each man's hand and greeted them warmly. "I've heard a great many things about you, Mr. Intissar."

"Good things I hope," he laughed, "and please call me Jason."

"Jason it is," David agreed. "Won't you sit?"

The older man nodded, and he and Garrett pulled up chairs. "So you're a pastor," Jason said rather thoughtfully, "I know we're here to deal with your brother's career, but I have a proposition for you as well, if you're interested."

David was curious. "I never overlook a chance for the hand of God to direct me. I'd be happy to listen to your ideas."

"Good man," Jason said as he waved to the serving girl. "How about some breakfast, Garrett?"

"Sounds mighty good to me," Garrett drawled. His wavy brown hair and boyish face made him seem young, but David was impressed by the way he handled himself.

The young girl took their orders and left the men to their discussion. Jason began the conversation by explaining his precarious health.

"My main interest in having a doctor nearby has been my own failing health. I have a bad heart, according to the doctor in Denver. I don't know what, if anything, can be done for me, but I'd feel a heap better having a regular doctor closer to the ranch than Springer or Cimarron."

"I see," Daniel said, then questioned, "where do you have in mind for my wife and me to live?"

"Well, of course it would be up to you, but I'd be happy to see to it something comfortable was built. Money isn't a problem. I can secure land for the house anywhere, but of course, I'd prefer it be in close proximity to my own land."

"How far from Santa Fe would that be?" Daniel asked, considering Katie's upcoming delivery.

"The ranch is a week away from Santa Fe. Is it important that you live near Santa Fe?" Jason questioned.

"My wife is due to have a baby in a couple of months. I'd feel better if we were somewhere close to another doctor. At least until after the baby is born." Daniel replied honestly.

"I don't see a problem with that," Jason

said with a smile. "It seems like a reasonable request."

"You know, Jason," Garrett suddenly spoke up, "you have that place about three hours from here on the rail line. Couldn't they stay there until we got another place built for them and Doc's wife has her baby?"

Jason's face lit up. "That's a wonderful idea, Garrett. We only use that place for shipping out livestock after roundup. What do you think about that, Dr. Monroe?"

"Three hours, eh?" Daniel was considering the situation.

"That ought to put you close enough, Daniel," David said, trying to encourage his brother.

"I suppose it would at that," Daniel said with a smile. "I believe we can work something out."

"Good, good," Jason said enthusiastically. "Now, how about the permanent house? Where do you think you'd like it to be?"

"It really won't matter after the baby is here safely," Daniel replied. "I suppose whatever you have in mind would be great."

Jason paused long enough in the conversation to accept his breakfast. "I thought a great deal about this," Jason said as he smiled broadly. "I'd like nothing better than to get a little more civilization near the ranch. Nothing real big, but something more than what we have. I'm even thinking of setting up a town somewhere close to the ranch. Perhaps your house could be my first step toward reaching that goal."

Garrett added with a laugh, "This has been Jason's dream for as long as I've known him."

"It sounds like a good one," Daniel replied.

"Now for you, young man," Jason said turning to David. "What I have in mind is a mission among the Pueblo Indians. A large Pueblo reservation is located near my property and it has been my desire to get the Word of God to these Indians. They are good folks, Mr. Monroe."

"Please call me David."

"They are good people, David. They have a love of the land and work hard to make life better for their people. I've been very impressed with their industrial spirit, but unfortunately, they have little or no interest in Christianity. That's where you would come in. I'd like to build a mission where you could live close to the reservation and be available to visit them on a regular basis and invite them to come to you."

"That's exactly what I feel God has called me to do," David said with such wonder in his heart he could hardly believe Jason's words.

Jason smiled and nudged Garrett. "God is good, Garrett. Just look at how He's blessed us today."

Garrett smiled, "That He has, Jason."

"So you will consider setting up a mission on my land?" Jason asked David seriously.

"I'd be happy to. I'll give it some prayer and reflection and get back to you."

"I'd have it no other way. Now, if you two don't mind, I'm going to give this plate of food my undivided attention," Jason said as he dug into the food.

David spent many hours alone in prayer that night. Excitement about Jason's proposal surged through him, and sleep was impossible. Turning through the Scriptures, David found a peace of mind he'd not realized was missing. He knew where he was being led, and rather than moving in a general direction, he had a specific mission to fulfill. God had given him his life's work.

As David settled down and turned out the lamp, he praised God for introducing him to Jason Intissar. Just before he fell asleep, his mind drifted to thoughts of Jenny Oberling. He could see her dark brown eyes so sweet and trusting. He could almost hear her gentle voice, and he longed to be with her.

Was Jenny also a part of God's plan for his future? She hated the Indians. She'd not yet learned to let go of the past, and she would never want a future that included living among the Pueblos.

To accept Jason Intissar's proposal and God's purposeful direction, David would have to give up Jenny Oberling. Yet, to choose Jenny over the mission work would be to turn his back on God. David sighed and pulled the covers over his head. What was the answer?

CHAPTER 6

"What's the hold up?" David called to the top side of the wagon.

Daniel peered over the canvas covering and grimaced. "If you think it's so easy to tie this load down, then you come up here and do it."

David laughed and walked away. "No thanks," he called over his shoulder, "I'll just go see if Katie needs anything."

"She'd better not have moved from that chair I put her in," Daniel shouted to David's retreating form.

David made his way to the hotel room and knocked loudly. At Katie's soft welcome, he opened the door and peered inside. True to her promise, Katie was sitting where Daniel had left her.

"Are you ready to go yet?" she questioned as she looked up from her needlework.

"Just as soon as that husband of yours ties one of his fancy surgical knots and gets the wagon tarp secured," David said with a grin. "How about you? Are you sure you're up to the ride? It's over six hours, you know."

"I'll be fine," Katie said as she put her sewing aside and struggled to get out of the chair. David went immediately to her side and offered his arm. "Thank you," Katie said as she steadied her ill-proportioned body. "I don't seem to be anything but awkward these days."

"No thanks necessary," David replied, "I'm just mighty excited about this new little one. How much longer do you figure before he'll be here?" Fearing he'd been too personal, he quickly added, "If you don't mind my asking."

Katie laughed. "Just because you don't discuss a woman's condition, doesn't make it go away. The baby is due next month."

"And, of course, my brother wants a boy," David said with certainty.

"Actually, he says he doesn't care either way as long as the baby is healthy. I guess I feel the same way," Katie said as she patted her rounded form. "Although, I am partial to the idea of a boy, myself."

"Me, too," David admitted.

Katie went to the window and looked out on the street below. "I never expected Santa Fe to be this large," she said as she watched the people hurrying on their way.

"Nor this beautiful?" David asked.

Katie turned and smiled. "Nor this beautiful. It really is a charming town. I'd never seen adobe before coming to New Mexico. I love the different colors."

"It's that way because of the various clays. They mix it with straw to make the adobe bricks. It's orange around here, but up at the Taos Pueblo village, Pastor Ed tells me it's more sandy brown. Other places it's almost pink," David offered by way of making conversation.

In truth he still wasn't as comfortable around Katie as he'd like to be. What he really wanted to talk to her about was whether she and Daniel had any interest in God.

As if reading his mind, Katie's expression turned quite serious. "You know, Daniel never told me you were a pastor. At least not until we were on our way down here. In truth, I don't think he knew you were here until your ma told him."

"I can well imagine. Daniel is five years older than me. When you're anxious to make the most out of life, you don't worry too much about leaving a little brother at home before you up and move off to college. I've never told Daniel this, but I was devastated when he left. He was pretty young, but he knew he wanted to go to college. I guess he never thought about what he left behind."

"Oh yes, I did," Daniel said as he came through the door. "I thought about it a great deal. Sometimes I thought about it so much, I nearly left college and came home."

"You never told me that," David said somberly.

"I know," Daniel replied as he came to embrace Katie. He held her against him for several minutes. "I never wanted to make you feel worse than you already did. Ma told me how hard you'd taken my leaving, and believe me, it wasn't easy to go."

David smiled. "But you're here now, and we won't be all far from each other, especially after my nephew gets here."

Daniel laughed heartily. "So you've convinced him that it's a boy," he said as he squeezed Katie's shoulder.

Katie looked up at her husband with wide-eyed innocence, "Who me?"

David grinned at the loving banter. "If you don't mind, we've got a long, dirty ride ahead of us. Pity we can't wait until they repair that stretch of track. I'd much prefer a three-hour train ride to six or seven hours of jostling cross-country."

"Me, too, but you heard the railroad man.

There's just no way of knowing how soon they'll be done. I'd like to be settled for Katie's sake," Daniel said and turned to his wife. "Are you ready, Katie?"

"As ready as I'll ever be," she replied with a smile.

"I think I'd better go check that tarp and make sure the doc here got it tied down properly." David interjected. Truth was, he missed Jenny more than he'd like to admit, and watching Daniel and Katie was a painful reminder of her absence.

The trip was grueling, and because of the rough terrain and deeply rutted trail, David and Daniel were forced to stop many times in order to give Katie much-needed rest from the jostling wagon. More than once, Katie chose to walk rather than suffer the bouncing on the wagon seat.

Nearly eight hours after they'd left Santa Fe, the small adobe house came into view.

The mountains rose to the north, and in the death that came with autumn, they added highlights of green pine and flaming vegetation to the desert brown and orange.

The air itself had an arid chill, although the early October sun did its best to warm the earth. As they drew closer, Katie could make out several flowering cactus plants that had been transplanted to grow along a cobblestone walk to the front door.

"Oh, it's lovely," Katie said as she turned to her husband. "I shall truly love living in this land."

David tied his horse to a small hitching post at the end of the walkway and went to help Katie down from the wagon. "Just wait until you see the inside, little sister. You're going to love it!"

"I already do!"

David opened the door and noticed Katie's wearied expression. "You must be exhausted. Come on over here and sit," he said as Daniel came up from behind.

"I knew this was going to be too much for you. Forget sitting. I want you in bed immediately," he said and easily lifted Katie into his arms. "It's a good thing David and I came out here ahead of time and got this place ready."

David opened the door to the bedroom and stepped back. "I'll fix some supper," he offered as Daniel deposited Katie into bed.

"That'd be great," Daniel called over his shoulder. "If it isn't too much trouble, how about bringing Katie a cup of hot tea while I start unpacking the wagon?"

"You don't need to wait on me," Katie argued. "I'll be fine in a few minutes."

"It'll be more than a few minutes before

you'll feel fine," Daniel laughed. "Now stay put and relax."

"That's right, Katie," David agreed, "I'd be happy to make tea for you."

It wasn't long before David made good on his offer and brought a steaming cup of tea to Katie's bedside. He helped prop her up, then handed her the cup.

"What made you become a minister?" Katie asked.

David was so surprised that he absent-mindedly sat down on the edge of the bed. "Well," he began, "I couldn't imagine being anything else. God's calling to me was so strong that when I tried to ignore it, He kept finding ways to get through to me."

"So you didn't want to work in the church?"

"It wasn't that," David answered softly. "It was more a concern that folks would think me pretentious. I mean, I was always rather serious. Daniel had the reputation of being the fun-loving brother. Me, I was always off spending time alone, thinking about my life and what I wanted to accomplish with the time I'd have here on earth."

"And what did you decide?" Katie questioned as she took a sip of the tea.

"I felt I had to show people there was

more to life than working and existing day to day. I wanted them to know the emptiness in their lives wasn't from a lack of things, but from a lack of God in their hearts. I wanted so much for them to know about Jesus and His sacrifice for us."

"You talk about God like you would about Daniel or me," Katie said, rather surprised. "I can't imagine feeling that way. I believe in God, but not like you do. God is important and powerful, and if you don't do what He wants, He punishes you, then you die."

David felt the need to share his heart, and in spite of his concern that he might alienate his sister-in-law, he plunged ahead.

"God is important and powerful," he began, "and if you die without repenting of your sins and accepting His Son, Jesus, as your Savior, you will be punished. But there is so much He offers us. So many good and enjoyable things, not the least of which is eternal life."

"I've heard people talk about living forever in heaven," Katie admitted.

"It's more than that, Katie," David tried to explain. "Eternity with God starts with your acceptance of Jesus as your Savior. You don't have to wait until you're dead to enjoy the benefits and peace that come from being a child of God."

"I'm not sure I understand," Katie said softly.

"Nor me," Daniel's voice called from the door. "I guess I've wanted to ask you some questions since we first arrived, but the time never seemed right."

David felt ill at ease. It seemed strange to be leading his older brother to an understanding of God. The thought of being his brother's keeper came to mind.

"Life can deal you some painful moments," David explained. "You won't escape those even as a Christian, but you can escape the worry and concern when those moments are upon you. It's a matter of faith. Faith in God to trust Him for the answers even when things are so muddled there seem to be no answers."

"Faith?" Katie questioned. "Faith in something you can't see or put your hand on? That's a lot to ask."

"It wouldn't be faith if it didn't require some sacrifice on your part," David said thoughtfully. "You sacrifice your control and worry. God's part is to do everything else."

"Seems unnaturally simple," Daniel replied.

"Not at all," David said with sudden revelation. "When somebody comes into your office with a broken arm, you know what needs to be done and you do it. You wouldn't allow the patient to dictate how you should fix the arm, would you?"

Daniel grinned and Katie laughed. "There's no way Daniel would allow anyone — especially his patients — to tell him how to care for his patients," Katie added before Daniel could answer.

"Why is that?" David questioned.

"Because I'm the doctor," Daniel stated firmly.

"But what about the fact they know better about their own pain?"

"That's sometimes the problem. Because of the intensity of their pain, they often don't realize what's necessary to get them past it," Daniel said, and it suddenly became clear where David was leading the conversation.

"And because of our pain, we don't always know where God is leading us. We can't know everything, but we don't have to. When we belong to God, He takes care of that just like you take care of doctoring your patients."

"But how can we be sure He'll listen?" Katie questioned.

"Jesus said, 'Ask, and it shall be given you; seek, and ye shall find; knock, and it shall be opened unto you,' " David said, quoting

Matthew 7:7.

"God wants to give His children good things, but He wants most of all to give them eternal life. In that same chapter of the Bible, Jesus said, 'Or what man is there of you, whom if his son ask bread, will he give him a stone? Or if he ask a fish, will he give him a serpent? If ye then, being evil, know how to give good gifts unto your children, how much more shall your Father which is in heaven give good things to them that ask Him?' "

"The key is to ask. God is only too happy to accept you into His family."

"I think I'm beginning to understand," Katie said as she nodded her head. "We can't expect God to help us if we don't let Him."

"Just like being a doctor," Daniel admitted. "If people don't come through my office door, I can't offer them my help."

"Exactly," David said with great relief. He'd thought it would be much more difficult to explain, but as Pastor Ed had often reminded him, he never worked alone. God was with him.

"So how do you get saved?" Katie asked. "Do you have to do something special for God?"

"God's gift of eternal life is free," David

replied. "We could never do anything good enough or great enough to equal the gift God offers. There's only one way we can have eternal salvation and that is to ask for it."

"That's all?" Daniel questioned in disbelief.

"Basically," David answered. "You must repent of your sins and seek to change your old lifestyle and ways. You must be willing to give yourself over to God and accept His help to start a new life."

"And if you do this," Katie stated, "if you really try to change and you honestly want to lead a new life, what happens if you stray or make a mistake?"

"Then you ask God to forgive you and you try again. God's grace knows no limits. Of course, you don't go out of your way to sin just so God can offer you grace and forgiveness."

"I'm not sure I can buy that," Daniel said thoughtfully. "I mean, how can God keep forgiving me? Won't He ever throw up His hands and give up on me?"

David chuckled despite the seriousness of the question. "You and Katie are going to have your own child soon. Say you tell your son or daughter they must stay away from rattlesnakes because they are deadly poisonous. And say you have an obstinate child who thinks he knows best and doesn't listen. If your child gets snake bit, will you take care of his wounds?"

"Of course," Daniel answered.

"What if he gets bit more than once?"

"I'd care for him as many times as it took. Of course, I'd sure be explaining the need for obeying the rules in the meantime."

David couldn't suppress a laugh. "We're no different, Daniel. God explains the need for obeying the rules by giving us His Holy Bible. But He also cares for us as many times as it takes and forgives us no matter how many times we mess up. His love is unconditional and unlimited."

"I want that," Katie said with a glow warming her face. "I want to have an eternity with a God like that."

Daniel turned to face his wife. "Me, too," he said with a sheepish grin.

David felt tears form in his eyes and felt no shame as they fell upon his cheeks. It was a moment so holy he could nearly hear the angels singing in heaven.

Taking hold of his brother's and sister-in-law's hands, David led them in a prayer of repentance. When they'd finished, all bore tears upon their faces and an afterglow of peace.

The next morning, Katie's strength had returned. She puttered around the house putting things in their place, not knowing how long this would be her home.

"You certainly have a way with things," David said as he came upon her in the kitchen.

"I love to have my things around me," Katie admitted. "The long preparation for coming here and for finding a place to stay has left me separated from my memory pieces far too long."

David fell silent as he wondered to himself how Jenny might set up a home.

"You miss her a lot, don't you?" Katie observed as she joined David at the table.

"What?"

"Jenny," Katie said softly. "You really miss her."

"Yes," David confessed. "I guess I didn't know it showed so much."

"Well, it does. Daniel and I have even discussed it."

"It's just her life is so bad, and she's so young. I wish I had an easy answer for the situation, but I don't," David said rather dejectedly.

"How does Jenny feel about you?" Katie asked as she eased her body onto a chair.

"I'm not really sure," David answered. "I think she enjoys my company, but I don't know if she feels more than friendship for me."

"Do you want her to?"

"More than I can say," David answered quickly. "I never realized until now, how much I want her to care. I love her, Katie. I love her, and I don't know what to do about it."

"Why don't you tell her?" Katie questioned.

"Do you really think I should? She's only sixteen, and she's not had a chance to meet many men or to court. I wouldn't want to rush her into something she might later regret."

"If you want my opinion, some folks are plenty ready at sixteen. Look at me. When I met your brother, I hadn't courted any other men, but I knew he was the right one for me."

"You certainly made a good choice," David admitted.

"Why don't you pray about it?" Katie asked with a grin. "That is what you'd tell one of us to do, isn't it?"

David laughed. "You're right, of course. I

need to commit this to God. After all, if Jenny does feel the same way and marriage becomes a possibility for our future, I would want God's guiding hand upon us."

"I knew you'd figure it all out. And," Katie added, "if my opinion counts for anything, I think Jenny has already lost her heart to you. In fact, I think when you get back to Santa Fe, she'll probably bring up the subject before you get a chance to."

David had never felt such hopefulness. "I pray you're right, Katie. I pray you're right."

Chapter 7

Jenny was quick to realize things had changed between Natty and herself. Natty had begun to watch her with discomfort and mistrust.

More than once, Natty had questioned her about young Pastor Monroe. Jenny was furious with Natty for her constant haranguing and endless tirades, but there was nothing she could do to stop them. She resented being plagued about her feelings for David, which grew stronger and deeper every day.

Jenny struggled to make it through the days and weeks that passed. From the first morning's light, she put her mind and body to work. She heated outdoor caldrons of water and watched in thoughtful silence as the steam hit the cold morning air. It had been over a month since she'd seen David.

She wondered as she moved clothes absentmindedly against the scrub board whether or not she should seek him out and explain her feelings. Jenny shook her head as if answering herself. No, David would just see it as a childish crush. There was no sense in tormenting herself with thoughts about a life with David.

Jenny was startled back into reality by heavy knocking on the kitchen door. Wiping soapsuds from her hands, she made her way from the courtyard and through the house.

Opening the door, she was surprised to find David. Any thoughts of what to say were wiped from her mind when she noticed the grave expression on his face.

"It's Katie," David said in a breathless voice. "Daniel sent word by train. She's having the baby and not doing well."

Jenny's forehead furrowed in worry. "What can we do?"

"I don't know too may people yet, and Pastor Ed is out making calls in the country. He's not due back until Saturday. I thought maybe you'd be able to go on the train with me to Daniel and Katie's."

"Me?" Jenny questioned.

"Yes," David said frantically, "Katie knows you, and it might comfort her to have your company. I know it would be a comfort to me, and I hoped you might agree to come along."

"Of course," Jenny said as she tried to

keep from shouting for joy. In such a grave situation, she didn't want to appear unfeeling. "I'll just get a few things."

"Daniel will have all the birthing things," David said as he wondered what Jenny could possibly think necessary to take.

"I know that," Jenny replied softly. "I thought we might need something to eat on the way. How far is it?"

"It'll be at least three hours by train," David said in a worried tone that caused Jenny to pick up her pace. "We'll take the spur from town and join the main line of the Atchison, Topeka, and Santa Fe about eighteen miles to the south. From there, it's another two hours north."

Jenny nodded as she pulled her heavy woolen shawl over her head and shoulders. "I'm ready," she said, handing David the bag she'd packed.

"Should you leave a note for Mrs. Morgan?"

"I suppose I should," Jenny conceded. She jotted a few words on a piece of paper and followed David out the door.

At the depot, a special train had been arranged for the express purpose of getting the pastor and his party back to the seasonal holding pens, which adjoined the property where Daniel and Katie had taken residence. The mood was set in the somber expression of the brakeman and conductor as David and Jenny climbed the stairs and took their seats on the short, four car train.

The train's crews had come to have a special affection for Mrs. Daniel Monroe. Every time they made water stops, Katie would come out and offer them cookies warm from the oven or pieces of her home-made pie. She'd won them over with her easygoing nature and laughing voice. Each crew member felt he owed a special debt to the tiny woman who would soon bring another life into the world.

The train had been stoked and was ready to make the trip before David had been notified, so it was no surprise when it pulled out before David and Jenny had taken their seats.

Jenny was thrown back against the hard wooden seat and stared open-mouthed as the scenery rushed past them. She'd never ridden on a train before, and the rocking motion was relaxing her against her will.

"Jenny," David's worried voice broke through her wonderment.

"Yes?"

"Will you pray with me?" he questioned as he took hold of her hand.

Jenny's heart nearly broke for the man

beside her. His concern was clearly etched in every line on his face. "Of course," she replied, wondering what he might expect of her.

David smiled slightly and squeezed Jenny's hand. When he bowed his head, she did likewise and waited in silence for him to speak.

"Father, I need You so much," David prayed in an earnestness Jenny had never heard voiced in prayer. "We all need You. We need You to go before us and be with Daniel and Katie as they work to bring their child into the world. Lord, only You know in Your sovereign wisdom what will happen, what may have already happened. Father, we want Your will and not our own, but we pray You will give us the ability to deal with that will, whatever it may be. In Jesus' name, amen."

Jenny had never before felt the emotions that flooded through her. There was something so powerful in the words David had prayed. She envied the ease with which he spoke to God and wondered if she could have it for her own.

David refused to raise his face for a moment. He relished the moment of prayer with Jenny. Even though she hadn't made a declaration of faith in Christ, he knew she was open to God's message for her heart. He hoped there was a future for them, and that he could spend the rest of his life in intimate moments before his God, with Jenny as his wife.

For hours they rode on, their hands still entwined. Neither made a move to change the situation, and neither spoke for fear it might cause the moment to pass.

Sagebrush and cactus passed outside the window. In the near distance, the snow-capped peaks of the Sangre de Cristo Mountains rose to break the barrenness of the desert. As the sun rose and its brilliance reflected from the icy mountaintops, the scene looked more beautiful than anything Jenny had ever known.

She braved a glance at David, who was watching her with renewed interest. Jenny met his eyes and felt her breath quicken. She loved him so much. There was no doubt about her feelings and no use denying them.

"David, I —" Her words were interrupted by the conductor bursting through the door.

"We're here!" he announced, grabbing the nearest seat as the train shuddered to a stop. The squeal of metal on metal caused Jenny to clench her teeth.

David quickly escorted Jenny off the train and onto the loading platform. The train would wait to take Jenny and David back to Santa Fe because no other passenger train would be through for several days.

It didn't surprise either David or Jenny that Daniel didn't greet them at the door. David gave a knock and walked in without waiting for any word from his brother. The house was quiet except for the crackle and pop of the wood stove, which obviously had been tended regularly.

David strode to the bedroom door and knocked again. His brother joined him in a heartbeat.

"Did you bring another doctor?" Daniel questioned as he looked around the room.

"No, I couldn't find anyone who could come with me. I thought maybe Katie would find comfort in having a woman at her side, so I brought Jenny."

Jenny's head snapped up in surprise. He'd called her a woman! David thought of her as an equal.

"I need a doctor!" Daniel said louder than he'd intended. Jenny could see the perspiration on his face.

"You are a doctor," David insisted. "You can do everything that needs to be done. Have a little faith in yourself."

Daniel ran his hand back through his sweat-soaked hair. "I don't think so, little brother. Katie isn't progressing the way she ought to be."

Jenny felt a sudden braveness and spoke. "May I see her?"

Daniel nodded and Jenny went quickly through the door and to Katie's bedside. She tried not to be surprised at the sight of Katie's near-lifeless form. Jenny reached for a basin of water and the cloth that lay beside it. Dipping the cloth in the water, she spoke softly and wiped Katie's brow tenderly.

Delicate lashes fluttered open as Katie drew a ragged breath to speak. "Jenny, how kind of you to come."

"Hush," Jenny whispered as she continued to bathe Katie's face. "I'm glad to be here. I know what a wonderful occasion this is. I wouldn't have missed it for the world."

Katie smiled weakly. "Where is Daniel?"

Jenny looked beyond the bed frame and through the doorway. Daniel stood speaking with David in hushed tones. "He's talking with David. Do you want me to get him?"

Katie shook her head. "No, please don't. I need to talk with you alone."

Jenny couldn't hide her puzzled expression. "With me? But why, Katie?"

Katie drew another deep breath as if it would strengthen her. When it didn't, she closed her eyes before continuing. "I'm not going to make it, Jenny."

Jenny wiped damp ringlets of blond hair away from Katie's face and forced a smile. "Of course you are, Katie. What nonsense. Every mother-to-be feels that way. You just wait until that baby is born. You'll see."

Katie reached up to still Jenny's lips with her fingers. Her hand fell weakly back to the mattress. "No," she said in a resolute manner. "You must listen to me, Jenny."

"Alright," Jenny said as she dropped the cloth into the basin and took hold of Katie's hand.

"Jenny," Katie's soft voice was barely audible, "the baby is dead."

"No!" Jenny stated sternly. "Daniel would have told us."

"Daniel can't think rationally, Jenny. He's been beside himself. I've been ill for two days now." Katie fell silent, and Jenny wondered if she'd lost consciousness.

"How do you know?" Jenny braved the questioned.

"The baby hasn't moved for hours," Katie began. "Daniel told me that they move less as they are born, but Jenny . . ." She paused. With added sadness in her voice, she spoke again. "I'm his mother, and I know he's gone."

Jenny felt tears in her eyes. "Oh, Katie.

I'm so sorry."

"That's not all, Jenny. I need you to be strong, and I need you to help me."

"I'll do whatever I can," Jenny answered. She felt a growing love for the young woman.

"I'll soon be joining my son," Katie said with exacting words. "I can't leave, however, unless I know you and David will help Daniel to keep his faith in God."

Jenny felt stabbing pain in her chest. "How can you be certain, Katie?"

Katie smiled sadly. "I can hear the singing, Jenny." Her face brightened. "I can hear all of heaven singing. Oh, Jenny, it's beautiful."

Hot tears fell against Jenny's cheeks.

"Are you afraid?" Jenny asked. She didn't hear the men as they stepped into the room. She clung tightly to Katie's hand and held it to her heart.

"No," Katie said with more surety than Jenny would have thought possible. "My son is there and my King."

Jenny couldn't suppress a sob, "Don't leave us, Katie. Please don't leave us."

"Don't cry, Jenny." Katie offered the comfort and it sobered Jenny as she remembered she was to be there for Katie's benefit.

"I'm sorry," Jenny said as she tried to

compose her emotions.

"Pray with me, Jenny," Katie pleaded with her last bit of strength.

"I'm not sure I know how," Jenny whispered, "but I'll try." She thought back to David's words on the train. She couldn't remember exactly how he had started, so she began in the only way she could. "God, I know we don't know each other real well, but Katie here knows You. Please God, don't take her from us."

"No," Katie whispered. "Pray for Daniel, not for me."

Jenny nodded, "Alright, Katie. God, please help Daniel. You know how much he's suffering."

"Please God, don't let my Daniel go astray. Don't let him grow bitter in my passing," Katie murmured. Jenny thought she heard someone leave the room.

Jenny opened her eyes and looked down at Katie's face. It was so delicate and pale, yet there was a peacefulness to her countenance Jenny couldn't explain.

"Thank you, Jenny. Would you please get Daniel? I want to say good-bye."

"I'll get him," Jenny whispered. She turned and found the room empty. David had gone ahead of her to retrieve Daniel.

Daniel was shaking his head as David was

trying to convince him to go to his wife.

"I can't watch her die," Daniel said angrily. "I've killed her. Isn't that enough?"

"You didn't give her life," David stated firmly, "and you can't take her life. She's in God's hands now."

"He can't have her!" Daniel shouted back.

"He already does," David whispered in contrast.

"Stop it!" Jenny said as she came forward and put a hand on both men. "Stop it right now! Argue and mourn your losses later, but right now, Katie needs us."

"I can't," Daniel said and his voice cracked.

"Yes, you can," Jenny said as she took control and pulled Daniel toward the bedroom. "You have to for her sake. She wants to say good-bye, and she needs to know you'll be alright."

Daniel looked deeply into Jenny's eyes. "But I won't be alright ever again," he whispered.

"I know how you feel," Jenny replied as she thought of her family. It was a moment only she and Daniel could share. David couldn't understand the loss they faced.

Daniel nodded and followed Jenny to his wife's bedside. Kneeling beside the bed, Daniel took hold of Katie's hand. Tears poured down his face. Jenny cried silently as she stood at the end of the bed. David's hands fell in support upon her shoulders, and Jenny felt warmth spread through her body.

"Don't cry, Daniel," Katie whispered.

"But I've failed you."

"No," Katie answered weakly.

"But I'm a doctor," Daniel said in sorrowed dejection.

"And I'm a woman. Have I failed you because I couldn't give our child life?"

"No!" Daniel said, suddenly sobering.

Katie smiled at her husband's stern expression. "And neither have you failed me, Beloved." Katie sighed and closed her eyes. "Thank you for loving me, Daniel, and thank you for our child."

"Oh, Katie! It's me who thanks you for the happiness I'd never thought possible," Daniel said as he leaned forward to kiss her one last time. "I love you, Katie."

"Do you hear it, Daniel?" Katie said as her expression brightened unnaturally.

"Hear what?" Daniel asked as he pulled Katie close.

"The bells. Those beautiful bells," Katie smiled and fell limp in Daniel's arms.

Daniel looked in shock from Katie's still

form to David's and Jenny's tear-streaked faces.

"Get out!" Daniel said firmly.

"You need us now," David said as he took a step forward.

"Your God did this. I asked you to pray for her to get well and you prayed for His will. Well, He's had His way and now I'll have mine. Get out and don't ever come back!"

"You don't mean that," David said in shocked horror.

"I do mean it," Daniel said as he narrowed his eyes. "Take her and leave."

"God will give you comfort if you allow Him to," David offered softly. "It's all a matter of faith. Trust Him, Daniel. He won't leave you alone in this."

Daniel gently placed Katie's body on the bed and got to his feet. He stepped forward in a menacing way that caused David to take a step backwards. "I said get out, and I mean it. I don't want your religion or your formulated answers for why my wife is dead."

David took hold of Jenny's arm and pulled her along through the house. Quickly, David retrieved their things and opened the door for Jenny.

Daniel stood firm in his anger at the opposite side of the room.

"I love you, Daniel," David said as he motioned Jenny through the door. "I'll always love you, and so will God."

Daniel's eyes narrowed. "That's not my problem. It's yours and God's."

CHAPTER 8

David and Jenny rode the rails to Santa Fe in stunned silence. They sat side by side, holding hands as if hoping to gather strength from their loss at Katie's bedside.

It was Jenny who finally broke the silence and sought an understanding of Katie's passing. "David," she whispered in the fading light, "are Katie and her baby really in heaven?"

David's head snapped up, revealing tearstained cheeks. "I know she is," he replied confidently.

"How?" Jenny questioned, needing to know.

"The Bible says so," David answered. "Remember when Jesus was dying on the cross?"

Jenny shook her head no.

"Jesus was condemned by His own people because they didn't understand who He was or why He'd come to them. Oh, there were a few who loved Him and knew Him for who He was, but they were too few to stop the others who wanted to put an end to His ministry. When Jesus was on the cross dying for the very people who'd condemned Him to death, two other men were being put to death. One man was only interested in having his flesh saved from death, but the other man was different. He knew Jesus was blameless."

"What did he do?" Jenny asked softly.

"He asked Jesus to remember him when He came into His kingdom. Jesus replied, 'To day shalt thou be with me in paradise.' That thief passed from life on earth to life in heaven with Christ."

"What about the other man?" Jenny asked.

"There is a passage in the Bible, Revelation 21:7–8, that explains what happens to people after they die: 'He that overcometh shall inherit all things; and I will be his God, and he shall be my son. But the fearful, and unbelieving, and the abominable, and murderers, and whoremongers, and sorcerers, and idolaters, and all liars, shall have their part in the lake which burneth with fire and brimstone: which is the second death.' "

"How awful," Jenny said.

"Yes," David agreed as he gazed out the window beyond Jenny.

"David," Jenny spoke, remembering Katie's peace in death. "I want to be saved from hell, and I want to know the same kind of peace and contentment Katie knew."

"I'm so glad, Jenny," David spoke, loving her more than he'd known possible. "Do you believe Jesus can save you from your sins and from the torments of hell?"

"Yes, I do."

"And you want Him to forgive you for your past sins?"

"Yes," Jenny replied. "I want that most of all."

"Are you willing to repent and turn from sinful behavior?" David questioned as he took hold of Jenny's hands. "Even your hatred of the Indians?"

Jenny grew thoughtful. "I don't know if I can forget what has happened, but I will seek daily to forgive the people who took the lives of my family. I certainly don't want to see any more killings happen. It won't bring back my family and it won't make my loss any less. But knowing I'm going to heaven when I die gives me peace I'll see my family again."

"I know God will help you, Jenny," David said with certainty. He led Jenny in a prayer of repentance and felt renewed hope for the future, even in the shadow of Daniel's rejection.

When David had finished praying, Jenny knew there would never be a better time to share her feelings for him. "David," she began, "there's something else I want to talk to you about."

David dropped Jenny's hands and leaned back against the seat. He was drained of all energy from dealing with Daniel, but Jenny seemed to offer him new vitality. "I'm all ears," he said as he turned to meet Jenny's warm gaze.

"I'm not very good at this," Jenny said slowly. "In fact, I've never done this before."

David raised an eyebrow curiously. "Go on," he encouraged.

Jenny took a deep breath and lowered her eyes. She twisted her hands in her lap as she struggled to choose the right words.

"I've never known anyone like you," Jenny began, "and I've never known the feelings you bring out in me." Jenny paused and wondered if she should continue. What if David didn't share her feelings? She'd have to endure another hour or more alone with him, and if he rejected her love, how would she be able to stand the closeness?

"And?"

Jenny sighed and realized there was no

reason to avoid letting David know any longer. "I've fallen in love with you, David. I suppose you think I'm too young to know what love is all about, but I do know, I know I love you. I can't stand it when you're away from me, and I feel so good when you're nearby."

Jenny was afraid if she stopped talking, David would say something negative and ruin the moment. She was also afraid to look at him and panicked when she felt him reach over and lift her face to meet his eyes.

Without warning, David leaned over and pressed his lips tenderly to Jenny's. There weren't adequate words to speak his heart, and his kiss was the only offering he knew would be capable of saying everything he felt.

When he pulled away, Jenny fell back against the seat and sighed. He hadn't rejected her. She waited in silence for David to speak.

"You are very young," David said surprising them both. "However, you are very wise and mature. I know you've had to endure a great deal in your life and it has aged you somewhat, but I worry that you've never had the chance to meet other men. Perhaps you only love me because you've never had the chance to know anyone else."

"No," Jenny said firmly. "I love you because you are the right man for me. I know God sent you to me for a purpose."

David said nothing for a few minutes, causing Jenny to fear he didn't share her feelings. "I know He did too," David finally spoke. "I love you with all my heart, Jenny. I have from the first moment I saw you rain-drenched and sorrowed, standing in the church not knowing what you were looking for."

"Oh, David," Jenny said and threw herself into his arms. "I was so afraid you'd tell me you couldn't love me."

David held her close, breathing a sigh of contentment against her ear as he buried his face in her long dark hair. "I will always love you. I pledge that to you now and forever."

"And I pledge my love to you, David," Jenny whispered. "Now and forever, wherever the journey takes us."

"Would you be willing to marry me?" David questioned. "Not right now, but in a year or two when you are a bit older."

Jenny couldn't hide her disappointment as she pulled away from David. "Why do we have to wait? People my age get married every day. Some are a lot younger than I am. I don't want to wait, David. After all,

I'll be seventeen in just a few weeks."

"I know all of that, Jenny," David said as he tried to think of just the right words. "I'm nearly finished with my studies and my apprenticeship with Pastor Ed. Jason Intissar, the man who hired Daniel to come to the territory and practice medicine, has a proposition for me as well. Frankly, I'm not so certain you would find it an appealing one, and I feel led to give it a try."

"What has he asked you to do?" Jenny questioned in a worried tone.

"Mr. Intissar wants me to run a Christian mission for the Pueblo Indians who live in the area up north of Santa Fe."

"Then you would leave Santa Fe and I wouldn't see you at all?" Jenny asked, trying to keep her voice even and under control.

"It would only be for a short time until I was able to get things going. Even though Mr. Intissar has kindly offered to provide everything, there is so much for me to learn. I'd need to learn the language just to be able to speak with the people. Then too, I'd need to learn their way of life and what they already believe about religion and God. There will be a great deal of work, and it wouldn't be an easy task under ideal circumstances."

"But I could help you. Don't you see? It

would be easier with someone at your side." Jenny tried her best to sound convincing. "I would be able to keep house, cook, clean, sew, and of course, do laundry," she said with a smile.

David couldn't help but laugh. "Of course." Just as quickly his smile turned to a frown as he thought of Natty Morgan. Her influence was bound to take its toll on Jenny's heart and soul. Could he in good faith leave the woman he loved in such a foul place?

"What's wrong?" Jenny asked, noticing David's frown.

"I was remembering Natty. She could be a bit of a problem. If she's expected you to provide for her all these years, she won't be likely to let you go without a fight."

"No, I don't imagine she would," Jenny replied. "But I don't care. I don't owe her a thing. These years with Natty have been spent in misery and pain. I've worked hard for her, and I deserve a life of my own."

"True," David said as he studied the young woman before him. "Still, if you agree to marry me and we wait for a spell, she shouldn't complain too fiercely."

"I wish you wouldn't insist on waiting," Jenny said and bit her lower lip to keep from saying more.

"But you will wait for me, won't you?"

Jenny rolled her eyes and sighed. "You aren't offering me any other choices, are you?"

David smiled as he gave Jenny's arm a squeeze. "The time will pass before you know it. Let's plan to marry when you're eighteen — that's only a little more than a year away. You'll need that much time to plan the wedding," David teased. "And while you wait, read this," David added and handed Jenny a Bible.

Jenny smiled. "Alright," she finally agreed. "I'll marry you when I turn eighteen, but I'm not waiting a single day beyond January 1, 1886." She glanced down at the book in her hand. "Thank you for the Bible. I'll probably have the whole thing memorized by the time you get around to marrying me."

"I'm so happy, Jenny. Thank you for understanding," David said as he pulled Jenny into his arms. "I promise you won't regret your decision."

Jenny laughed and turned her face to David's. "I've no doubt you're right," she murmured as he lowered his mouth to hers in a passionate kiss.

When the train finally pulled into Santa Fe, it was well past nine o'clock at night. David walked Jenny to her home, enjoying the time they shared together, but in his heart was the sorrow that Katie was dead and his only brother had alienated himself from David's support and love.

As they approached Jenny's home, David noticed Natty peering out the window. "You'd better let me explain," David said, opening the gate for Jenny and leading her up the walk.

"Why bother?" Jenny questioned. "She won't be understanding, and she won't care what the excuse is. Natty will only know her meal wasn't on the table and her friends lacked refreshments while gambling at her home."

"I should at least try," David insisted.

Jenny opened the door. A string of curses filled the air, and Natty yanked Jenny away from David's tender touch.

"Where have you been?" Natty yelled. "How can you call yourself a man of the cloth and allow a child such as this to be compromised?"

"I beg your pardon, Madam," David began, "Jenny hasn't been compromised in any way. My sister-in-law went into labor and my brother sent word that help was needed. We took the train to their home north of Santa Fe. We were under constant supervision."

"What possible need would a woman giving birth have for this child?" Natty screeched.

"They were friends. I thought Jenny might offer comfort and support," David responded evenly. "And I might add, she did."

"Jenny doesn't have time for friends," Natty said in a calmer voice. "I don't believe your story, young man."

"It's true, Natty," Jenny said having grown tired of the confrontation. "I've never lied to you, and I'm not lying now. Katie Monroe died a few hours ago. She was my friend for only a short time, but nonetheless, she was my friend. She and her baby now live in heaven."

For once, Natty had run out of words.

Jenny continued, "David, I think you should leave now. I'll see you tomorrow."

David nodded and moved toward the door.

"No, you won't!" Natty said in an ominous tone. "You are not to come here again, young man, and you are never to see Jenny again, anywhere, at any time."

"You can't control her life forever," David said as he narrowed his eyes. He moved toward Natty, then hesitated and turned toward the door. "I intend to make Jenny my wife, and there isn't anything you can do about it. She doesn't belong to you, and she isn't going to work herself to death in order for you to be waited on. I love this woman — obviously something she hasn't enjoyed since the death of her parents — and you will not separate us."

"You are very wrong about that, Sir. Very wrong," Natty said and crossed the room, putting herself between David and Jenny. "I'll have the law here if you aren't off my property immediately, and if you dare to show your face here again, I'll personally shoot you between the eyes."

Jenny gasped and moved forward. "You leave him be, Natty. I've done nothing wrong, and you can't treat me as if I were a child. David, please leave. I'll be fine. I have to talk with Natty, and it would be best if you weren't here."

David nodded and moved to leave. "I assure you of one thing, Madam," he said as he filled the doorway with his full height. "If you harm Jenny in any way, you will answer to me and answer dearly." With that he was gone, and Natty was left to slam the door behind him.

Natty turned, red-faced, to confront Jenny. "I've offered you a home and food for your belly, and this is my thanks?"

"You've offered me nothing," Jenny said,

willing to brave Natty's rage. "I've worked myself into exhaustion to keep this place and to provide the food we eat. You spend your days and nights in gambling and all types of depraved entertainment. I've endured it for years, but enough is enough. I intend to find other living accommodations tomorrow!"

Jenny stormed off to her room before Natty had a chance to reply.

Natty sat down on a chair. In mild shock, she began to formulate a plan. There was no way she'd allow Jenny Oberling to slip through her fingers without receiving some kind of return on her investment. The first order of business would be to confine Jenny.

Before first light, Natty promised herself, there would be a lock firmly in place on Jenny's door. A lock on the door and bars on the window if necessary, Natty determined with a smile. Whatever it took to keep Jenny locked inside and David Monroe out.

CHAPTER 9

Natty sat shrouded in the darkness that was the inseparable companion of her favorite gambling house. The man sitting opposite her at the poker table was impeccably dressed and obviously wealthy. He was also a man of worse reputation than any other who tormented Santa Fe.

"You say she's nearly seventeen?" the man questioned as he raised a glass of whiskey to his lips.

"Yes and *untouched*," Natty added.

"Are you certain of that?" the man asked, leaning forward and narrowing his dark eyes in a menacing manner.

"I'd stake my life on it. I checked out the pastor who's been keeping her company, and he's got a better reputation than Archbishop Lamy himself," Natty said referring to the beloved archbishop of Santa Fe.

The man nodded and smiled. "And she's not a mixed breed?"

114

"No," Natty insisted. "She's white."

"Well, if what you say is true, I have a customer who'll pay quite nicely to take your niece off your hands. We have a marriage auction coming up on the fifteenth of January. Can you have her in back of the San Miguel Mission by nightfall?"

"I don't think she'll come willingly."

"We have many reluctant brides," the man said as he reached into his silk vest pocket and pulled out a vial of liquid. "Just put this in her water or coffee. It won't knock her out completely, but it will make her easier to handle."

Natty took the vial and smiled. "And when will I get my money?"

"At the auction." The man finished his whiskey and got to his feet. Giving a slight bow, he left.

Jenny's captivity had passed from days into weeks, until finally she realized she'd missed both Christmas and her birthday. Natty had locked her in her room and hired a man to install bars outside the windows.

Jenny thought she'd go mad trying to free herself. First she'd tried to break down her door, but Natty had called upon one of her associates to reinforce the frame with metal bars similar to those on Jenny's windows.

Jenny had screamed for help, but Natty had threatened to have her moved out of town to stay with one of Natty's friends. Jenny had no desire to be left to the care of the desperate characters Natty called friends, so she remained silent, even when she heard David in the foyer.

As the weeks passed, Jenny spent most of her time praying God would give David the direction and wisdom needed to defeat Natty. But as the sun set night after night, Jenny grew fearful and frustrated.

"Dear God," Jenny murmured, kneeling beside her bed one night, "I know You're watching over me because David said You'd never leave me alone and if I belonged to You, You'd hear my prayers and answer them. Please God, please help David to save me from Natty and whatever plans she's making for me. You have the power over evil and power over Natty Morgan, so please deliver me from this place. Amen."

Jenny got to her feet, blew out the lamp, and got into bed. Thoughts of David and his gentle love filled her mind. Would she ever be reunited with him? David had told her trust and faith formed the key to peace in God. "I trust You, Lord," Jenny said as she closed her eyes. "I trust You."

■ ■ ■ ■

David paced the floor, reviewing Jenny's predicament. He wished he knew Natty's plans, but the few times he'd gotten past her front door, David had been showered with a tirade of Natty's obscenities that revealed nothing of her intentions.

A sharp knock at the door interrupted David's thoughts. Outside stood Garrett Lucas.

"Evening," Garrett said as David opened the door to him. "I'm Jason Intissar's foreman, Garrett Lucas."

"I remember you," David said as he stepped back. "Come on in and take a load off."

"I'm not usually given to interfering in other people's business, but there are a couple of things I thought we ought to talk about. The first is your brother and the second is your lady friend."

"Jenny? What do you know of her?" David questioned anxiously.

"Well, it's not pleasant," Garrett said, removing his black Stetson and accepting a chair David offered.

"Coffee?" David asked as he poured himself a cup.

"Please," Garrett replied and fidgeted with his hat until David held out the steaming cup. Putting his hat on the empty chair beside him, Garrett took a long drink. "Hits the spot," he sighed.

"You surely haven't come all the way from the Intissar ranch tonight, have you?" David observed as he took the seat opposite Garrett.

"No, I've been staying at your brother's place. That is, until yesterday. I took the train down and have a room over at the Exchange Hotel."

"How is Daniel? I've been quite worried, but he refuses to see me. I've sent several letters to him, but he won't have anything to do with me. He blames me and God for Katie's death."

"I know."

David studied the man before him. He seemed so young. How strange that Garrett would be the one to bring him news of Daniel.

"Does Daniel talk to you?" David asked painfully.

"At first he didn't, but we've come to be real good friends over the past few weeks. I didn't know about the baby and his wife when I first showed up at the house. Daniel wouldn't open the door to me, but after I slept two nights in the barn, he figured I might freeze to death and invited me to sleep in the house."

"What were you doing there?" David questioned.

"Jason had sent me. I was supposed to be checking up on Daniel and Katie, as well as getting Daniel's decision on several possible places for his permanent home. Only now, I guess there won't be a permanent home."

"What do you mean?" David asked, nearly dropping his cup.

"That's why I came to see you. Daniel plans to pack up and move. He said as much as he loves New Mexico, he can't bear to stay where Katie's grave stares him in the face every day."

"But he doesn't need to stay there. Didn't Mr. Intissar want him to move closer to the ranch anyway?"

"That's what I reminded him of. I think I've talked him into coming up to the ranch until spring. I wanted you to know he'd be moving in case you came looking for him," Garrett replied with his eyes downcast.

"Daniel told me he wasn't on speaking terms with you," Garrett continued. "We've talked a great deal about Katie's death and how he blames God for it. I'm a Christian, myself, and I've tried to explain trusting

God in the bad times, but your brother is determined to see this as a personal attack. I shared Romans 8:28, telling him God works all things together for good for those who love Him, but your brother looks at me like it's all some cruel joke. I wish I could reach him. Maybe in time, I will."

"I'm grateful for what you've done," David said, getting to his feet. "I wish I could see him. No, actually I wish he would see the truth. I know how he's suffering. Well, not exactly, but enough I feel I could offer some love and support. I want to be with him, but he won't allow me to."

"Don't be too hard on him," Garrett said. "Daniel will come around in time 'cause he's too smart to do otherwise. Just have faith, Pastor." He grinned.

"You're right, of course," David returned the smile. "It's just I've never been good at waiting. I mean, the situation I'm facing with Jenny Oberling is a good example. That reminds me, what do you know about her?"

"I'm afraid my news about Miss Oberling isn't encouraging. Fact is, it's quite the opposite. Jenny is in grave danger, and I knew you'd want to know. I'll help you any way I can."

David paled considerably. "What do you mean?"

"I happened across some information and learned it involved Jenny. I already knew from talking to Daniel you had hopes of marrying her, so when I heard she was to be involved in an illegal marriage auction, I knew it most likely wasn't of her own accord."

"Marriage auction? What's that?" David asked, knowing it seemed like a ridiculous question.

Garrett pushed his cup back and sighed. "It's mostly a front for white slavery and prostitution. Girls think they're bargaining for a husband, but most often they're signing away their lives into all types of heinous activities. No doubt your Jenny isn't going of her own free will, but that doesn't matter to the men who run the auction. As long as the women are provided, they will run their trade."

"I'm certain Jenny would never agree to this auction," David protested, sitting down in a chair opposite Garrett.

"What are we to do?"

"You love her, right?"

"Of course, I do. I asked her to marry me on the trip back from Daniel's. She loves me as much as I love her. I've been praying and biding my time." David buried his face in his hands. "Now it would seem I've waited too long."

"You gonna give up, just like that?" Garrett questioned. "I know I wouldn't let the woman I love get away without a fight."

"What do you suggest? I've been to talk to Natty Morgan — she's the woman who's holding her captive. I've tried to talk sense to her, but she won't listen."

"Does Natty ever leave the house?"

"I suppose," David said as he raised his face in hope. "What do you think we should do?"

"I can watch her house," Garrett suggested. "After all, she doesn't know me. I could keep an eye on her, and when she's going to be out, I could come after you. You could come break in and take Jenny out."

"It might work," David agreed as he got to his feet once again. "I can't thank you enough for coming to help me. I would never have known in time and Jenny might have . . ." His voice trailed into silence. "Well, I don't want to think about what might have happened. We won't let it happen, and that's all there is to it."

"Then we're agreed," Garrett said as he stood and put his hat on. "Give me directions to her house, and I'll start watching immediately."

David walked to the door with Garrett.

"Our best chance will probably be at night," he decided. "Natty used to do most of her sleeping during the day and spend her nights partying at one establishment or another."

"Then I'll go straightway from here to their house," Garrett said as he stepped into the night darkness.

"You're a good man, Garrett Lucas, and I hope we can be friends for a long, long time."

Garrett smiled and nodded in agreement.

"Now, as for the directions," David said, "you turn left at the corner and head two blocks north. You'll turn left again at the next corner. Her house will be the second on the right."

"Sounds easy enough," Garrett said and buttoned his coat against the cold. "I'll let you know when it's clear."

David watched Garrett disappear into the darkness. He got the strong impression he and Garrett were just beginning their relationship. Despite his youth, Garrett Lucas would make a good friend.

CHAPTER 10

David's opportunity came the following evening. Around midnight, long after David had given up hope of seeing Garrett, he appeared at the door breathless.

"It's time, David," Garrett said as David tried to pull on his boots. "Mrs. Morgan has planted herself in one of the south side gambling houses. She doesn't look inclined to return home anytime soon, but I suggest we hurry."

"I'm with you all the way," David said, pulling on his coat. "We'll come back here after we get her, and Pastor Ed will marry us. That way, Natty won't have a chance of getting Jenny back."

"You can come to Jason's ranch with me afterward," Garrett insisted. "Since Jason wants you to set up a mission, for the Indians, this would be perfect timing." David nodded and followed Garrett into the street.

By Jenny's calculations, it was January 14. She had passed over two months in captivity. Instead of breaking Jenny's spirit, Natty Morgan had only managed to steel her determination to escape.

Jenny had taken to matching Natty's sleeping habits. While Natty ventured away each night, Jenny worked at putting a hole in the wall that separated her bedroom from the sewing room. Natty would never step into the sewing room, and Jenny knew her only chance of escape would be through that wall.

Jenny sighed as she pounded away at the thin, but stubborn, wall. She had taken the brass candelabra and used the base to chip away at the wood. "Lord, give me the strength I need," Jenny whispered. She repeated Philippians 4:13 again and again for encouragement: "I can do all things through Christ which strengtheneth me."

Natty had been gone little less than an hour when Jenny heard noises coming from downstairs. She stopped her pounding and listened. Natty was returning. Jenny's heart sank as she put the candelabra back on the nightstand. Hearing scuffling sounds on the steps, Jenny returned the unlit candles to the candelabra and sat down on her bed.

She waited in silence, wondering why Natty had returned so early. It surely couldn't mean anything good. Her heart pounded harder as the footsteps on the stairs came closer. She pulled her knees up to her chest and held her breath.

Bang! Bang! Bang! The door was still reverberating from the pounding when Jenny called out in a weak voice. "What do you want?"

"Jenny! It's me, David!"

"David!" Jenny called as she raced to the door. "Oh, David, is it really you?" She leaned her face against the door as if it would bring her closer to him.

"It's really me. I'm here with a friend, and we've come to break you out."

"You'll never get through this door," Jenny said, "but I've been trying to break through the wall that joins my room to the sewing room. If you go in there, you might be able to get me out. It's the room to the right."

"We'll give it a try, Jenny. You be sure and stay clear," David called.

"I will," she agreed and moved across the room to where a single candle was burning on a small table.

Jenny could hear the men move supplies

and furniture in the sewing room to reveal the small hole she had put through the wall.

"This ought to be fairly simple," Garrett said as he motioned David to stand back. It took only three powerful blows of Garrett's booted foot until the wood splintered and cracked. Both men reached down and pulled the boards away until a hole large enough for Jenny was created.

"Bring whatever you can't bear to leave behind, because I don't intend for you to ever return," David said in an authoritative voice that gave Jenny strength.

Jenny hurried to put her meager wardrobe and family mementos into a bag. The last thing she reached for was the beloved Bible, which had become her mainstay. Placing it in the bag, she handed it through the opening into David's waiting hands.

"Just put your head and shoulders through the opening and we'll lift you out," David said as his heart raced in fear. Too much time was slipping by, and his concern that Natty would return was haunting his every move.

Jenny popped her head through the opening and a broad grin spread across her face. "I've been working at this for weeks, and you come along, put a little pastorly persuasion into it, and here we are."

David reached out and took hold of Jenny's shoulders. "It wasn't me," he said as he eased Jenny through the hole. Garrett cleared away debris that blocked her path.

As the men got Jenny to her feet, she immediately threw herself into David's arms. "I wouldn't have cared if Indians themselves had come to take me away. Thank you so much," she said with tears pouring freely down her face. "I wasn't sure you'd come for me."

David took hold of her face and kissed her wet cheeks. "You must never doubt my love for you, Jenny. Never, never doubt that my love binds me to you. Because of it, we can never truly be separated."

Jenny nodded and reached up to push back David's blond hair as it fell across his forehead. "I will never doubt it again," she whispered.

Garrett cleared his voice uncomfortably. "I hate to break this up, but we need to get out of here before Mrs. Morgan returns."

David dropped his hands and Jenny turned abruptly to face her other rescuer. "Thank you so much for helping us," Jenny said as she leaned forward and kissed Garrett's boyish cheek. "I thank God for the both of you."

"I, too, thank God, Ma'am, but we needn't

put Him to a foolish test. I suggest we leave by way of the courtyard," Garrett drawled as he picked up Jenny's bag and led the way.

Jenny let David pull her along through the darkened house, hardly daring to believe the joy that rushed through her. She was being set free — free from a life of misery with Natty Morgan and free from the fear of losing David.

Once they'd reached the courtyard and alley, Jenny let go of David's hand in order to pull her skirts up and nearly fell into a hole. David took hold of her arm to steady her.

When they were nearly a block away from Natty's house, David and Garrett slowed the pace to a brisk walk. Jenny's pounding heart steadied and her breathing evened. "Where are we going?" she whispered into the dark night.

"The church," David responded.

Standing safely in the vestibule of the Methodist Church, Jenny felt as if the nightmare she'd lived the past weeks was nothing more than a dream. She waited patiently as David exchanged a few words with Garrett before disappearing through the sanctuary of the church and into the back rooms.

Garrett tossed his Stetson onto one of the

pews and put Jenny's bag beside it. "You're a lucky woman," he said as he gave Jenny a lazy smile.

"I know," Jenny agreed and returned the smile.

"By the way, I'm Garrett Lucas."

"I'm indebted to you, Mr. Lucas," Jenny said as she extended her hand.

"Just plain ol' Garrett is good enough for me," he said as he took her hand. "I kinda figure after you and David move to the ranch, we'll become pretty good friends."

Jenny's eyes grew wide in surprise. "What are you saying?"

Garrett frowned for a moment. "I just figured you . . . well, I thought . . ." Garrett's embarrassment was evident.

"Don't worry about it, Garrett. You haven't caused me any problem. Please don't feel bad."

"Why should Garrett feel bad?" David asked as he came through the back door with a sleepy-eyed Pastor Ed.

"I'm afraid I let the horse out of the barn, so to speak," Garrett said, raising his eyes sheepishly to meet curious stares. "I mentioned something about you all moving to the ranch."

David laughed. "Is that all? Jenny, I know this is short notice, but Pastor Ed here has been good enough to get up in the middle of the night and marry us. If you're willing, that is," David said softly.

Jenny looked contemplative for a moment. "Are you sure it's the best thing for us?"

"Are you afraid it might not be?" David questioned.

"No. I feel confident in your choices. I'd love very much to marry you, David." Jenny's smile was all the reassurance he needed.

"Well," Ed said with a yawn, "if you two are agreed, I'd really like to get on with this."

David laughed and pulled Jenny with him to stand in front of Ed. "Then let's get to it. We wouldn't want Natty Morgan to come busting in and ruin our plans."

Jenny stiffened noticeably, and David offered her a comforting smile. "She's not going to ruin our plans, Jenny. Don't worry. God is with us in this."

Jenny nodded, and Pastor Ed began the ceremony that would join the two young people together for the rest of their lives.

Twenty minutes later, David and Jenny Monroe followed Garrett Lucas on horseback. They rode north to a new life serving God. It was the tenderest journey Jenny had ever embarked on, and her heart held a deepening love and admiration for the man she now called husband.

CHAPTER 11

Spring 1893

Jenny Monroe brushed on the final touches of whitewash and stood back to survey her work. Three small graves gleamed from the outlines of whitewashed rock. There were also whitewashed crosses at the head of each grave; faithful reminders that her children dwelt in heaven with their Creator.

Wiping the final smudges of paint from her hands, Jenny picked up her things and moved toward the adobe barn. Children's laughter rang sweet from the open pasture behind the two-story adobe house. Glancing out across the fields, Jenny counted the children.

One, two, three — her eyes continued their search until she counted seven. Jenny laughed as the children played the games David had taught them. He loved these young waifs as much as she did. Many had come to them as sickly babes — some as the results of epidemics that claimed their parents' lives — but all of them had one thing in common: they were Indian.

Jenny loved them as much as the three little ones she'd borne and buried. They were God's blessings.

When the children caught sight of Jenny, the sky filled with little brown hands waving with glee. To some, Jenny was the only mother they'd ever known, and they loved her as if they'd belonged to her forever.

How many children had crossed the steps of the orphanage and mission she and David tended? Jenny thought back over the years she and David had worked to establish their ministry with the Indians.

She had to laugh to herself as she went back to work. She had once hated the Indians, blaming them for the death of her family. Now she was mothering seven of them and working with the tribe of local Pueblo. God had been so good to her, but the transition hadn't come without a price.

Within the first four years of her marriage to David, Jenny had developed a strong, sustaining faith in God. She devoted herself to prayer, and each time she'd found herself with child, her faith and belief had been sorely tested.

She remembered the anticipation and

longing both she and David had shared as they'd awaited the birth of their first child. Having witnessed Katie's death not long before, they'd also been anxious about the delivery. When birthing day came, Jenny survived. Her baby did not. Jenny would never forget the devastation and heartbreak of burying that little babe who'd never known the sunlight on his face.

To watch their fears be realized had taken its toll on Jenny's and David's renewed hope. He realized he wouldn't lose Jenny as Daniel had lost Katie. The experience also helped him understand why Daniel's despair had so easily turned to bitterness.

Jenny's emotional recovery was much slower, however. She sat for hours in the room that would have been the nursery. Sometimes she cried, other times she ranted, but finally she accepted the event, remembering Romans 8:28: "All things work together for good to them that love God . . ." She still wasn't sure what possible good could come from the death of a baby.

Jenny looked heavenward. The skies had threatened rain all morning and yet the billowy black clouds hung overhead as stubborn sentinels refusing to yield their posts. *We could use a bit of rain,* Jenny thought as she moved across the yard. Her garden was just starting to show wispy shoots of green.

Jenny reveled in the change across the land as winter became spring in dusky hues of mint green and flowering white. It wouldn't be long until spring burst upon the scene in a riot of color and warmth, but for now she was content with the beginnings of life.

Back in her kitchen, Jenny busied herself with the necessary tasks at hand. She checked her roast, then the clock. David would be returning soon, so Jenny rang the bell to call the children.

Everyone had their jobs to do, and from the oldest to the youngest, each child knew what was expected. Jenny maintained if you had the ability to walk and hold onto things, you were old enough to help. Even three-year-old Storm, or Night-That-Storms as the Pueblo called him, was an able-bodied worker and happily carried the napkins and place mats to the table.

Jenny took pride in the children God had loaned her. Some would stay for years, while others were quickly retrieved by family members who'd learned of their fate. Jenny hated to see any of them go and was always happy to see David or one of the Pueblo people appear with yet another needy bundle.

"Is anybody home?" David called out as he came through the front door. Squeals of laughter filled the air, and all the children found hiding places. This was their nightly game, and no one would dream of doing anything different.

Jenny stood in the hallway, arms outspread. "I can't find the children. It seems they've disappeared again."

Giggles and the sound of hushed whispers could be heard throughout the first floor of the Monroe house.

"Mrs. Monroe, it would seem you are always misplacing them. I suppose," David said as he feigned exhausted reluctance, "I shall have to find them for you."

Jenny smiled and her brown eyes danced with love. For nearly ten years she'd been blessed enough to call this man husband, and every moment of her life she only loved him more.

"Ah-ha!" David shouted, and six-year-old Fawn screamed out in pleasure. David tickled her stomach and put her on one of the long table benches. "So, White-Fawn-Dancing, just where are your brothers and sisters?"

"Don't know," Fawn giggled, displaying the wide gap where her two front teeth were missing. "They're hiding. You won't find them."

"Oh yes, I will," David said as he raised the edge of the tablecloth to reveal three laughing toddlers. "Come here, you three." David reached his arms out wide and pulled the children to his chest. He whirled around once before putting the children on the bench beside Fawn.

"More!" all three yelled in unison.

"Not yet," David laughed. "There're still three more to find."

"I know where day are," Storm said in his baby-like voice.

David tousled his ebony hair and said, "Then you may help me." Storm smiled broadly.

Jenny watched the game continue and basked in the warmth that filled her heart. The only thing she was missing was a baby of her own. Quietly, she turned away from the group and finished putting the food on the table. She didn't want the children to see the tears that were in her eyes.

"Please Lord," she prayed in a whisper, "please let me be satisfied with that with which You have blessed me." She could hear the laughter in the front room and forced herself to concentrate on the happy voices of her husband and the orphans.

It should be enough, she realized, but just as readily she knew her discontentment ran deep.

"Papa David told me to help," Raining Sky said as she took a bowl of green beans from the kitchen counter.

"Thank you," Jenny said, composing herself and bestowing a warm smile on the ten year old. Jenny brought the roast and followed behind Raining Sky.

"Oh good," David called. "Come along, children. It's suppertime."

The little ones gathered around the table and joined hands as David led them in prayer. "Dear Father, we thank You for the wonderful meal which You have provided. We thank You too, for the children who share this food and the love they give us. Bless us all and help us to serve You all the days of our lives. Amen."

"Amen," Jenny agreed, and the children echoed her reply.

"Let's eat," David said as he started cutting the roast. "Pass your plates, and I'll put some meat on them."

"Don't want befajewels," Storm said and made a face.

"They're called vegetables, and you will eat them because they help you to stay healthy and strong," Jenny said firmly.

"Don't like 'em," Storm pouted but, nonetheless, took the offered plate of food.

Later that night, Jenny sat alone in the darkness listening to the silence of the house. The children were all asleep and even David's even breathing signaled he was deep in dreams.

"Why am I struggling so much with this, Lord?" Jenny whispered. "I love the children You've given me to care for. I don't mean to seem ungrateful, because it's not that I don't love my life. I just can't explain what I feel inside. It's like an incompleteness, a longing for that which I've only glimpsed from afar. I want a baby, Lord. A baby of my own that won't be taken up to heaven before I can share my life with him or be retrieved by the Indians to join his real family. I'm like Hannah before Eli in the temple: if You will but give me a child, I pledge to give him back in trust to You. But please, please Lord, let me love him on earth for a time."

CHAPTER 12

Several weeks later, Jenny stood admiring her garden. The beans were up high enough to merit staking off the ground, and the onions had already yielded a nice addition to their meals. Jenny leaned over and pulled a few weeds before going into the house to finish her baking.

Spring had come in wet and cold, and Jenny was grateful for the warmth of her toasty kitchen. She pulled two brown-crusted apple pies from the oven and quickly filled the emptiness with five tins of bread dough. Checking the clock, Jenny gauged herself to have time enough to whip up a batch of David's favorite Mexican custard before he'd return for lunch.

A ruckus of children's voices brought Jenny quickly from the kitchen to see what the problem was.

"Look," Fawn called out as she pulled Jenny toward the front window.

Jenny looked out across the front yard to see David approaching with three Pueblo men. She immediately recognized them as members of the council that guided the tribe in all its decision making.

"You children stay here and continue working on your studies. I'll check your work when I come back," Jenny said as she went to meet David. Jenny had only known the tribal leaders to leave the village when it was a matter of grave concern. She knew this time would be no different. She watched as David talked intently with the men, not even pausing to recognize Jenny's approaching form.

Jenny met them at the gate and noted the apprehension in David's eyes. "What is it?" she asked, uncertain she wanted to know.

David cast her a sorrowful glance. "They've come for the children, Jenny."

Jenny swallowed hard. This kind of thing had happened before, but usually the relatives of the children came — certainly never the elders. "Which ones?" she asked hesitantly.

"All of them," he lamented.

Jenny's mouth dropped open in shock. "All of them?"

"I'm afraid so," David said as he put his arm around Jenny's shoulder.

"But . . . but . . . ," Jenny stammered as her eyes filled with tears. "Why?" She looked at each of the tribal leaders with questioning eyes. "Why are you taking them away?"

"Sickness has taken many of our people," the oldest leader spoke.

Jenny recognized him as the *cacique,* religious leader of the Pueblo. "Black-Cloud-Raining, why do you want to take all of the children? If there's been sickness, won't they be exposed as well?"

"Many children dead. My people are fewer each year. They die from white man's fevers and walk the way of our father's to the spiritland. We need the children to make us strong again," Black-Cloud-Raining spoke firmly.

The *t'aikabede* raised his hand to speak before Jenny could comment on Black-Cloud-Raining's words. She respected the man whose word was ultimately the deciding factor. As the head of the tribal council the *t'aikabede* would never have left the village if the situation hadn't demanded his guidance.

"We would not have come without many talks. We spent many hours in the Kiva, praying and speaking of what we should do. We know that it is good for the people of our village if we bring the children home."

Despite the fact Jenny knew the religious significance of gathering in the circular adobe Kiva, she couldn't endure the pain in her heart. "But they have a good home here," she protested as her eyes filled with tears. "They belong with us."

"They are Pueblo and they belong with the people of their fathers," Black-Cloud-Raining said with little concern for Jenny's tears.

Jenny opened her mouth to speak again, but David shook his head sadly. "I've already said all of this, Jen," he offered painfully. "They are determined to take them, and we are powerless to stop them."

Jenny looked with pleading brown eyes to each Indian leaders'. She prayed silently that one would take pity on her and leave one or two of the youngest for her to care for. "Surely the littlest ones could stay," she said hopefully.

"No," the *t'aikabede* said firmly. "We will take all the children to their people. We leave now."

"At least let them eat. They haven't had lunch yet," Jenny said as the men moved toward the house.

"They eat while they journey." Black-Cloud-Raining's stern voice and expression caused Jenny to realize she was powerless. How could she stand by and watch them take away her children? How could God let this happen?

"I'll get them ready," Jenny finally said with a heaviness in her voice David hadn't heard since the death of their last child. "You wait here."

Jenny wished she could find it in her heart to offer refreshments, but she felt the old feelings of anger toward Indians creep into her heart. "Let them die of thirst!" she thought and immediately regretted her animosity. "Forgive me, Father."

Jenny called all the children into the foyer. "I have some news," she said trying to sound calm. There was no need to share her grief with the children. "Your families have asked the elders to bring you home. They have come to take you back to the tribe."

"We be gone long time?" Fawn asked, in her wide-eyed, innocent way.

Jenny's resolve nearly crumbled. "I'm afraid so, Fawn. The *t'aikabede* has come to take you home for . . . for . . ." Jenny's voice cracked as she struggled to force out the word. "Forever," she finally managed.

"Will we see you and Pastor David again?" one of the other children asked.

"Yes, of course you will. Pastor David goes often to the Pueblo village, and I will come with him to visit you," Jenny explained.

"Where will we live?" Fawn asked curiously. It was all starting to sound like a game to her.

"You will live in the adobe pueblos your people have built. Remember? We talked about the houses they live in. They are much like this house, only there are no doors or windows on the ground floor, or at least very few."

"It is to make our people safe," one of the older boys insisted.

"Yes, that's right," Jenny agreed. "You will live a different life there. You will not study from books as you do here. You will not speak English as much as you will the language of your people. Your jobs will be different, also. You boys will do more hunting and fishing, while your sisters work the hides and gather berries and wood."

"I make dem, too," Storm said as his little grubby fingers reached up to pull at Jenny's hands.

Jenny lifted the small boy in her arms and buried her face against his. "I know you will make your people proud," she whispered. "I know all of you will. Now, come give me a hug."

Jenny was rushed from all sides by the children. Even the oldest boy felt no shame in offering affection for his temporary guardian. "Now, go pack your things. The elders are waiting."

Jenny listened as the children's footsteps echoed up the stairs to their bedrooms. She could hear their pat, pat, pat down the hall as they ran in excitement. Why couldn't they seem less excited? No, Jenny reminded herself silently. She and David had worked diligently to teach the children they were to look forward to returning to their people. It would be wrong to expect any different from them now.

She took slow and deliberate steps to climb the stairs to where the children were excitedly chattering about their journey. She helped Storm to secure the small pack he would wear on his back. He looked too little to carry anything for himself, but Jenny knew the elders would expect no less. That was why she and David had always worked to teach the children the Pueblo way. She continued to remind herself it was for just this day they had worked so long and so hard. The children should be with their people to learn and preserve their heritage.

She monitored their packing and helped them to distribute their loads evenly so their little backs wouldn't grow sore. *Children should be cherished and pampered,* she thought, but even as she did, Jenny realized being too soft could prove deadly for these children.

There was a small, parade-like procession back down the stairs and to the front door. Jenny kissed each child and offered some tidbit of advice or reminder of a memory they'd shared together. When she picked up Night-That-Storms, it was all she could do to keep from running — running until she was so far away that no one, not the *t'aikabede* or Black-Cloud-Raining or anyone else, could take him away from her.

"I wuv you, Mama," Storm said in his babyish voice, forgetting to add Jenny's name. She was the only mother he'd known. Would he be upset to leave her?

"I love you too, Night-That-Storms. You are a Pueblo boy with a big heart. Don't ever forget me," Jenny said as hot tears fell upon her cheeks.

"Don't cry, Mama," Storm said, wiping at Jenny's wet cheek.

"Don't cry," Fawn said as she tugged at Jenny's arm. "You say this is good."

"It is good, Fawn. It's just I will miss all of you so much." Jenny put Storm down and composed herself. "Now, go and tell

Pastor David good-bye, and be sure and remember your prayers. Don't forget Jesus loves you and God is your Father in heaven." The children promised and went running out the front door to find David.

Jenny watched as David held each child, even the older boys. He held his face close to theirs, talking in low whispers as if imparting some great secret wisdom upon them. In truth, he was praying a blessing over each one.

"Bless you, White-Fawn-Dancing. May God watch over you all the days of your life. Don't forget you are loved and God sends His angels to watch over you and walk beside you," David said in a strained voice. He tickled her one last time just in order to hear her little-girl giggle.

"You funny, Pastor David. I love you."

"I love you too, Fawn," David said and suddenly felt old. He put Fawn down and finished blessing the others.

The leaders signaled it was time to go, and because of the respect the children had been taught by Jenny and David, they quickly fell into place. They walked out the gate and past the stone wall, some so in awe of their tribal elders they looked afraid. Others seemed oblivious to the older men.

Jenny ran to the gate in order to watch

the children as far as she could. The wind picked up and pulled at the strands of her chestnut hair she had so carefully pinned up that morning. She didn't care. As the children marched away, they took her heart and the security she had enjoyed in the face of her losses.

Jenny cried openly as she pulled open the gate and walked the length of the fence to better view the children as they neared the rocky canyon that would block them from her eyes. From time to time, one or more of the children looked back at Jenny and David, offering a wave or a smile. It was a great adventure to them.

As one after the other disappeared into the canyon, Jenny could no longer bear the silence.

"Don't take them. Don't go," she cried out, knowing they were too far away to hear her words.

David put his hands upon her shoulders, but Jenny wanted no part of it. She jerked away and moved forward as if to go after the children. She had taken only three steps when three-year-old Storm turned from the procession and ran back a few steps towards Jenny. He held wide his baby arms and threw out his chest, sending Jenny an open-armed hug he usually reserved for things he couldn't touch.

Jenny sobbed and collapsed to the ground as she mimicked Storm's actions. Her arms ached for the feel of his soft skin and satiny hair. She longed for his baby smell and his constant, questioning voice.

Storm, satisfied he'd shared his best with Jenny, turned and ran to catch up with the others. He didn't look back again, and for this David was grateful. Jenny had fallen headlong into the sandy dirt, releasing in her sobs all the pain David felt tearing at his own heart. Lovingly, he picked her up and carried her back into the house.

Placing Jenny gently in the bed, David did nothing to stop her from crying. She needed to mourn the loss of these children just as she had mourned the loss of her own babies. Walking quietly from the room, David made his way to his study and collapsed in a chair.

"Oh Lord," he cried, "this sorrow is too much to bear alone. Deal mercifully with us, Father." David reached for his Bible and opened it to Psalm 88: " 'O Lord God of my salvation, I have cried day and night before Thee: Let my prayer come before Thee: incline Thine ear unto my cry; For my soul is full of troubles: and my life draweth nigh unto the grave. I am counted with them that go down into the pit: I am as a man that hath no strength.' " David closed the Bible.

"I am that man, Lord. I am without strength. Jenny needs me to be strong, Father, and I have no strength to offer her. Help me to accept this as Your will and to ease Jenny's pain. Amen."

Long into the night, David could hear Jenny's sobs. He worried for her sanity. Surely it was too much for one woman to endure all she'd lived through.

When her crying could no longer be heard, David made his way to their bedroom. He undressed silently and slipped into bed beside Jenny's spent form. He pulled her into his arms and held her tightly. Somehow they would endure this as they had the other sorrows in their life. He was reminded of Psalm 30:5: " 'Weeping may endure for a night, but joy cometh in the morning.' " The words comforted David as he drifted into a fitful sleep.

Surely joy would come in the morning.

CHAPTER 13

Joy didn't come in the morning. David found Jenny a silent, stoic reminder of the previous day's events. She got up before David awakened, stoked the stove, and made breakfast, and put on water in the outside caldron for the laundry.

David dragged himself down the stairs after a restless night. He was amazed at all Jenny had accomplished, yet the sight of his wife was shocking. Her eyes were void of life. When he sat down to the table, she silently served him his food and left the room.

David thanked God for the food and asked Him for guidance and peace in dealing with the loss of his family. He couldn't explain to Jenny the pain he felt; it would only add to her burden.

He choked down his breakfast and started his day. The livestock needed to be fed, and their water trough was almost empty. It took several trips to the pump outside the back door for David to finish filling the trough.

David didn't mind the physical labor. It gave him something to keep his mind occupied. Memories of the children laughing and singing as they worked at their chores kept intruding. The morning work always seemed to pass quickly with the sound of their small voices.

From time to time, David cast a glance across the yard and saw Jenny working at some task. When he discovered her carrying two heavy buckets of milk, David rushed to her side and offered a hand. Jenny glanced up long enough to shake her head and pushed past David.

Unable to bear the silence any longer, David decided to go to the nearby town of Bandelero. He went in search of Jenny to see if she'd like to accompany him on the five-mile trip. He found her at the wash caldron, preparing to wash what was left of the children's clothing. Tears threatened to spill from her eyes, but she held herself aloof even as David embraced her from behind.

"I thought we could use a break from the quiet," he said softly, giving her shoulders a squeeze. "I'm going into Bandelero to get some of the things we need. Why don't you ride along and visit with Lillie?" David knew how much Jenny had come to love his brother's second wife.

David himself planned to speak with Daniel about Jenny. He was grateful the Lord had brought Daniel back into the fold. David remembered the day Daniel and Lillie had shown up at the mission after working with the Pueblos during a measles epidemic. Daniel had found his way back to God and had sought David's forgiveness for the separation that had occurred at Katie's deathbed.

Jenny stood silently looking beyond David as if she hadn't heard the question.

"Go on and get your shawl," David encouraged softly. "This laundry can wait."

"Yes, it can wait," Jenny said with anger. "It can wait because the children will never wear them again."

"Now, Jen," David said as he tried to turn Jenny into his arms.

"Leave me alone," she said in a quiet, deadly voice. "Go to town and visit with whomever you like, but leave me alone!"

David started to speak but realized the effort would be futile. He turned and walked away, more downcast than he'd ever been. How would they get past this situation if Jenny wouldn't share her grief?

Instead of hitching the wagon, David

chose to saddle his favorite horse. A long, hard ride would do them both good, he thought as he patted the gelding's neck. Lifting his boot to the stirrup, David swung into the saddle and urged the horse into a gallop.

Bandelero had grown considerably in the five years since Garrett Lucas, now owner of the Intissar dynasty, had put the first building in place. Garrett had lost his beloved mentor, Jason Intissar, to the devastating sickness that had prompted Intissar to request a doctor's presence in the first place.

Through the years since first meeting David and Daniel Monroe, Garrett had come to be good friends with both. David knew Garrett had tried to convince Daniel to stay in the territory after the death of his wife Katie. Both David and Garrett had felt the loss when Daniel rode out of their lives. Through the years that followed, Daniel had sent very little information about himself their way, and when it did come, it was always addressed to Garrett. The separation had grieved David, and only through Jenny's prayerful, loving companionship had he been able to concentrate on his ministry with the Indians.

But eventually, Daniel had returned. His

arrival had coincided with the appearance of Lillie Johnston Philips. Lillie had been a stubborn one, David remembered, but not nearly as stubborn as Maggie Intissar, Jason's daughter.

David nearly laughed out loud as he reined the horse to a trot. Maggie Intissar had made them all jump through more hoops than anyone cared to admit. At eighteen, she'd come on the scene after years of separation and alienation from her father, only to learn Jason had chosen Garrett Lucas to be her husband. Garrett had had no complaints, but Maggie had been livid.

David was still laughing when he reached his brother's office and home. Sliding off the horse, David tethered the gelding at the hitching post and offered him a brief stroke on the muzzle before going in search of Daniel.

Daniel met him at the door. "What are you laughing about, little brother?"

David paused for a moment. "I was just remembering when Maggie and Lillie first arrived. Maggie in particular. Of course," David said as Lillie appeared from the back room, "Lillie was just as much a cause to be reckoned with as her friend ever was."

Daniel laughed as Lillie appeared with

their two-year-old son James, attached to her skirt. "I'd say that's putting it mildly," he said ruefully.

"What are you two talking about?" Lillie questioned, lifting the boy to greet his Uncle David.

David quickly took the boy and received a wet kiss in greeting. It was the grandest welcoming he'd had all day. "I was just remembering you and Maggie when you were younger, more stubborn, and harder to manage."

"Who says she's any easier to manage?" Daniel asked teasingly. Lillie raised a questioning eyebrow to meet the challenge, but Daniel simply pulled her into his arms and kissed her into silence.

David loved the closeness Lillie and Daniel shared. He'd truly wondered if it would ever again be possible for his brother to love another woman after Katie. Then God had sent the recently widowed Lillie into Daniel's life, and the man hadn't been the same since. Both Daniel and Lillie knew what it was to lose a mate and a baby, and it was easy to see that God had put them together to bring healing into each other's lives.

"Where's John?" David questioned as he looked around for Daniel and Lillie's four year old.

"Where else would he be?" Lillie laughed. "He's at the creek watching the fish."

"Me too!" James squealed as he wiggled in David's arms.

"Well, if you two will excuse me," Lillie said, taking James from David, "I will take my son down to the water so that he might see the fish, also."

As Lillie retreated down the path to the small creek that ran through the town of Bandelero, David's face betrayed his mood.

"You might as well come in and spill your guts," Daniel said, pulling David into the office. "I'm sure Lillie left coffee on the stove. How about a cup?"

David nodded and followed Daniel through the office and into the adjoining quarters the family called home. He accepted both the offered chair at the kitchen table and a steaming cup of coffee.

"Thanks," David said mechanically.

"So, what's the trouble?" Daniel asked cutting through all the formalities.

"I'm not sure where to start," David said honestly.

"Is something wrong with Jenny?"

"No. Yes. But I'm not sure it's anything a doctor can fix. The elders of the Pueblo tribe came and took the children away yesterday. They took all of them, Daniel, and Jenny couldn't bear it. In truth, I can't say I'm handling it any better than she is." David put the cup down and sat back dejectedly.

"I see," Daniel began, "and why did the Indians come for the children?"

"You know they're just recovering from an epidemic of grippe. Because they lost so many children, they felt it necessary for the survival of the tribe. They came back with me from my visit and insisted the children return with them to the village. It destroyed Jenny. She fell apart watching the children leave and hasn't been herself since."

"Would you like me to come and give her a sedative?" Daniel asked.

"I doubt she would talk to you, much less take any treatment. She barely spoke to me this morning."

"Perhaps she'd talk to Lillie," Daniel offered.

"Maybe. Do you think Lillie would mind?"

"Would I mind what?" Lillie asked as she came into the kitchen with her children. The boys jumped onto their father's lap, full of excitement about the fish they'd seen at the creek.

"Look, boys, we adults have some prob-

160

lems to discuss, and I need you to go to your room and play. You can tell me all about the fish when I get done here."

"Go along now, boys," Lillie said as she joined Daniel and David at the table. "Now, tell me what you need me to do."

Lillie reined her horse to a stop atop the small hill that overlooked David and Jenny's home. She wanted so much to offer Jenny comfort, yet she wasn't sure what she'd say when she came face to face with her dear friend.

"Please Father," Lillie prayed, "please let me help Jenny through this pain. I don't know how You want to use me in this situation, but I trust You to lead me. Give me the strength and the wisdom to know what to say. Amen."

Lillie led the horse down to the house. She looked around for any sign of Jenny, but saw nothing, not even smoke from the caldron fire where David had left her earlier that morning.

Lillie tethered the horse at the barn and began to call out. When she didn't find Jenny in the barn, Lillie went to the house. She opened the door and called inside.

"Jenny! It's me, Lillie. Jenny, where

are you?"

Lillie walked from room to room on the first level, calling and praying Jenny would answer.

The house was as still as a tomb. Lillie felt her skin crawl. "Jenny, answer me!"

Lillie had just started up the steps when Jenny appeared at the top of the staircase.

"What do you want?" she asked Lillie softly.

"I wanted to come and be with you. David told us what happened. I thought maybe you could use a friend," Lillie said as she motioned to Jenny. "Come on and talk to me. Are you hungry? I can make us something to eat."

Jenny stood frozen at the top of the stairs. "I'm not hungry and I don't want to talk. I think you'd best leave now, Lillie."

Lillie started up the stairs. "Jenny, you shouldn't be alone. I know how much you're hurting right now. Please let me help."

"You don't have any idea how I feel. You have your family, your children. I have nothing."

"You have David and Daniel and me. Not to mention Garrett and Maggie. And what about John and little James?"

"You don't understand!" Jenny screamed.

"They took my children. Nothing else matters. Nothing at all."

Lillie tried to remain calm. "Jenny, please come down and talk to me. I know we can work through this together. God won't leave you alone in this, Jenny. Remember all the wonderful things you told me after I lost my baby?"

"I don't want to talk," Jenny said dispassionately. "Now, please leave. Please understand, Lillie. This isn't the time. I can't talk now."

Lillie nodded, remembering only too well how it felt to have everyone pushing her to explain her pain. After the death of Lillie's first husband, Jason Philips, and the death of their unborn baby, Lillie hadn't wanted to speak to another human being again. And she certainly hadn't wanted anyone telling her about God's sovereign wisdom and unending love.

"I love you, Jenny. Remember that. When you are ready to talk, I'll be there. Until then, I'll hold you up to God in prayer and wait."

"Thank you, Lillie," Jenny said. She turned and retreated up the stairs.

Lillie's heart grew heavier as she returned to her horse and mounted for the ride home. "Oh God," she pleaded, "please help

Jenny. Help her to find her way back from the pain. Please Lord, please."

CHAPTER 14

When David returned home he said nothing to Jenny about the way she'd dismissed Lillie. He knew how worried Lillie and Daniel were, but there was little he could do to change matters.

Jenny said nothing to him when they went to bed that night, but when he reached out to hold her, she pushed him away and hugged the far side of the bed.

How much longer could he stand Jenny's anger? He'd tried to share evening devotions with her, only to have her get up and walk away. When he'd suggested they pray over the evening meal, Jenny had complied with indifference.

"How can I help her, Lord?" David prayed. He tossed and turned throughout the night and finally gave up trying. He slipped downstairs and was still sitting at the kitchen table reading the Bible when Jenny came down to cook breakfast.

David ached to hold her. He was only beginning to realize how much he needed her to help ease his own pain.

Mechanically, Jenny poured David fresh coffee and placed a platter of hotcakes within his reach. She reluctantly sat down at the table and waited for David to offer grace as he had before.

"Jenny," he began instead, "please don't punish me for the children's absence. I didn't want them to go any more than you did."

Jenny stared at him. Lavender circles shadowed her brown eyes, and her cheeks were bloodless.

David continued, "I know we'd feel better if we worked through this together. Would you like to go with me to the village? We could visit the children and see how they're getting along."

"Why torture yourself, David?"

At least they were civil words, David thought. They gave him the courage to continue. "It wouldn't be torture to assure ourselves they're happy, would it?"

Jenny picked absentmindedly at the crocheted tablecloth.

"Jenny, did you hear me? I think it would be good for us to visit the village. We could leave right after breakfast, maybe even spend a day or two with the Pueblo."

Jenny got to her feet. "Maybe it would offer you comfort, David. To me it would only be a mocking reminder. And what of when we leave the village? It would be good-bye all over again. No," she said as she pulled her apron off and went to the back door, "you do what you have to, but don't ask me to subject myself to that kind of pain. I think it's cruel of you to suggest such a thing."

"Cruel?" David asked incredulously. "I honestly thought if you saw them happy and well cared for, you might get on with your life. You know it wasn't just the children who needed you. I need you, too."

Jenny stared at her husband. She wanted to rush into his arms and forget her pain, and for a moment she nearly did just that. She could hardly bear the anguish in his eyes. He was trying so hard to help her. Why couldn't she let go of her anger and allow his closeness?

"God will get us through this, Jenny," David whispered breaking Jenny's spell. She grimaced at the words. That was exactly why she was shutting David out. Just as Daniel had turned him away when Katie had died, Jenny was turning him away at the loss of the Pueblo children. It wasn't David she was pushing away, Jenny realized sadly; it was God.

Jenny turned, opened the door, and walked out. Wandering aimlessly, she found herself at the graves of her children. It had been more than seven years since she'd felt life grow inside her. Jenny's hands automatically fell to her flat stomach. The ache in her heart threatened to bring tears, but she pushed back the urge to cry.

Lovingly, she knelt by the three little graves. The whitewash was holding up well and the constant care Jenny had given each grave was evident. She had planted flowers, and with the warmth of spring quickly turning to summer, they offered an enchanting display of color. Jenny reached down to pull out stray weeds and was so intent on her job she didn't hear David come up behind her.

"I'm packed," he said softly. "I figure I'll be gone a few days. Will you be alright?"

"I'll be fine," Jenny said without malice.

"Are you certain you won't come along?"

Jenny dusted the dirt from her hands and got to her feet. She wanted to make things right with David, yet she couldn't explain the wall she'd placed between them. "I think the time alone will help me a great deal. I'll try to put all of this behind me by the time you get back."

"Will you kiss me good-bye?" David questioned, his face betraying his fear of her rejection.

"Of course," Jenny said and opened her arms.

David held her close for several minutes.

Jenny felt her resolve melting and feared having to face David's questions again. She pulled back slightly and placed a quick kiss on David's lips. It wasn't enough for David. He pulled her back into his embrace and placed a long, passionate kiss upon her lips.

Jenny stepped away breathless. She was amazed at the power David had over her. She didn't want him to leave, but she feared the outcome if he stayed. She turned back to her work at the graves and murmured a good-bye when David promised to return in a few days.

"Remember, if you need anything, Daniel and Lillie are only as far as Bandelero," David said.

"I'll remember, but I won't need anything. I'll be just fine."

Jenny listened to the sound of David's horse galloping across the yard. She lifted her face and watched David disappear into the canyon. When she'd been a young bride living at the Intissar ranch, she'd watched David leave to work with the Pueblos as he

169

established his ministry. Those days had dragged on endlessly until a puff of dust on the horizon revealed her husband was coming home.

Refusing to remember anything more, Jenny buried herself in work and unnecessary cleaning. At night she went to sleep too tired to feel the emptiness of the big bed she'd always shared with David, and in the morning the routine started all over again.

On the third morning after David's departure, Jenny awoke to the silence of an empty house. Instead of getting up and dressing for the day, she lingered in bed thinking about all that had happened. Although she fought it, Jenny was unable to ignore God any longer.

"God," Jenny announced in complete frustration, "I don't want to pray. I don't know what I want to do, but I know I don't want to pray." She waited for a few minutes, hoping the feeling would pass. When it didn't, Jenny threw back the covers and got to her feet.

She paced the wood floor of her room for several minutes before continuing. "I've trusted You all these years, and while it hasn't been easy at times, I always felt Your presence and comfort. But this time I feel numb and betrayed. Does that sound strange?" Jenny paused a moment as if waiting for an answer.

She caught sight of her disheveled image in the mirror. She hardly recognized the woman who stared back. Her long brown hair hung lifelessly around her shoulders, and her usually fresh complexion was sallow.

"Why?" Jenny raged as she swung away from the mirror and threw back the curtains from the windows. "Why must I continue to believe You can make this right, Lord? Why can't I forget what I know to be true? Why can't I walk away from my commitment to You?"

Jenny fought the urge to get the Bible on the nightstand. Why was God forcing her to reconcile things between them?

Unable to resist any longer, she opened the Bible to Lamentations 3:22: " 'It is of the Lord's mercies that we are not consumed, because His compassions fail not. They are new every morning: great is thy faithfulness. The Lord is my portion, saith my soul; therefore will I hope in Him. The Lord is good unto them that wait for Him, to the soul that seeketh Him. It is good that a man should both hope and quietly wait for the salvation of the Lord.' "

Jenny put the Bible down. These were the

same verses God had led her to after the death of her first baby. She contemplated them, remembering the pain of dealing with the death of her child. She'd been so young, and David so hopeful.

" 'It is of the Lord's mercies that we are not consumed,' " she repeated. She had relied heavily upon those words.

Jenny resumed her pacing. Forcing herself to remember her first delivery, she thought of how difficult the labor had been and how all she could concentrate on was the thought of holding her new baby. That baby had never taken her first breath. A tiny, silent girl had been laid to rest in the sandy soil in back of the newly constructed mission house.

Jenny remembered not only the devastation, but also her faith that God was with her. She had mourned for a long time, but within months, she'd learned she was expecting another child. Certain she'd faced the worst, Jenny had begun to anticipate the birth of her child without fear.

The second child, also a girl, had come more easily but much too early. Jenny had held the lifeless baby only a moment before they'd taken her away and buried her. Jenny had been too weak to attend the simple funeral. Her body had slowly healed, but

Jenny had not been as accepting of the will of God.

Jenny remembered her feelings at that time well: anger, doubt, betrayal. She had pummeled God with her questions: Didn't her choice to serve Him mean He would protect her from harm and pain? If not, why trust Him?

But in the face of losing her Indian children, Jenny's spiritual maturity wouldn't allow those questions to be raised again. She understood God often led His people through the fire in order to purify them.

Jenny's thoughts turned to the last of her children. A son had been born with a healthy, enthusiastic cry, and Jenny had rejoiced with David, confident God had blessed them with a child at last.

Within hours, however, Jenny had been devastated for a third time. Her newborn son had stopped breathing. Jenny had once told Lillie Monroe there hadn't been a shred of pride or arrogance left inside her after that experience. Lillie had wondered how Jenny could trust God after the death of yet another child, and Jenny had replied simply, "How could I not?"

Jenny's pacing stopped in front of the mirror. She tore her mind from its memories and faced the present. "I must go on trusting," she declared to her reflection. "David and I should have leaned upon each other and upon You, Father," she whispered. "David tried to help me and I sent him away; now You are all I have, God. At least for this moment."

Jenny picked up the Bible and flipped through the pages until she came to Psalm 51:12: " 'Restore unto me the joy of Thy salvation; and uphold me with Thy free spirit. Then will I teach transgressors Thy ways; and sinners shall be converted unto Thee.' " Jenny prayed the words as she read.

Putting the Bible aside, she got dressed with renewed strength. She wished David would come home so she could explain to him she was sorry for the way she'd acted. She still ached for the halls to resound with the voices of children, but at least those children were still alive and she would see them again.

Jenny got busy with her chores and was in the barn finishing the milking, when she heard the unmistakable sound of voices. Thinking perhaps Daniel and Lillie had come to check on her, Jenny picked up the buckets of milk and made her way to the front yard.

She rounded the side of the house and

came face to face with three Indians. Jenny immediately recognized them as Apache by the markings and clothing they wore. She screamed, dropped the pails of milk, and turned to run.

When a brave caught up with her and grabbed her arms, Jenny couldn't stop screaming. She was caught in the past — a ten-year-old girl, watching her family be cut down by Apaches. Blind with rage, Jenny scratched and kicked to get free.

The brave hit Jenny hard across the face. She knew only blackness as her body went limp. The brave threw Jenny over his shoulder and made his way back to his companions.

One man led David and Jenny's matched bays from the barn. The brave who held Jenny threw her across the back of one of the bays and tied her securely. He issued several quick commands and waited while his men ransacked the house and barn. Smoke betrayed the fact they'd set fire to the buildings.

Jenny began to stir, causing the leader to call out to his companions. The men came running with sacks full of provisions which they tied onto the other horse. The leader directed one of his braves to ride and the other to run alongside. He then mounted

behind Jenny's unconscious form and gave
a bloodcurdling yell.

CHAPTER 15

Jenny was jarred into consciousness by the constant thud of her ribs against the bare back of the horse. Her mind demanded she protest, but Jenny forced herself to remain calm and silent.

They were moving at a good clip across the canyon floor, and with every misstep the horse made in the rocky soil, Jenny became only too aware of the Indian who shared her mount.

At the words of the leader, the horses were slowed to a walk. Finally, they stopped altogether. Jenny hoped her captors would take her down from the horse, so she pretended to be waking.

Her moans caught the attention of the leader. He jumped from the horse and untied Jenny's bonds. As gently as Jenny would have handled a newborn, the Indian brave lifted her from the horse's back and set her feet on the ground.

Jenny forced herself to focus on her captor's face. The hateful dark eyes she'd expected were absent. In their place were eyes full of compassion. He spoke to her in Apache, but Jenny knew only a few words and couldn't reply. He switched to broken English, but the result was worse. Jenny finally asked the brave if he spoke Spanish.

"Sí," he replied.

Jenny breathed a sigh of relief which abruptly ended because of a wave of nausea. The constant jostling of the ride had been too much for her stomach. She dropped to the ground and vomited until she could scarcely breathe. Pale and gasping for air, Jenny was grateful for the water offered to her by the Apache leader.

She knew he was making a great gesture. The Apache prized water above all else. Under normal circumstances, hostages weren't allowed more water than was necessary to keep them alive.

Jenny rinsed her mouth and drank deeply from a canteen she recognized as her own. Feeling marginally better, she struggled to her feet and steadied herself against a rock.

"Muchas gracias," she said as she handed the canteen to the leader. "I'm Jenny Monroe."

The man eyed her for a moment, took the

canteen, and secured it around his neck before speaking. "I am called Two Knives by the N'de."

"Who are the N'de?" Jenny braved the questioned.

"The N'de are the people, the Apache," he replied.

"I know of no Apache reservations for a hundred miles or more. Where do you live?"

"Beyond the big river," Two Knives said. Jenny nodded, knowing he meant the Rio Grande. "We used to roam the land of our fathers without the white man's laws. Now N'de must live as animals in a cage on white man's reservations."

"But you're still raiding." The words were out before Jenny realized. She silently prayed she had not provoked Two Knives's anger with her words.

"My grandfather refused to be counted on the reservation. He thinks N'de sell their souls for rancid meat and white man's wickiup. N'de cannot hunt, cannot dance the dance of their fathers, and cannot walk the land the One-From-Whom-All-Things-Come gave to them." Jenny opened her mouth to reply but one of the braves signaled the approach of danger.

Two Knives clamped a hand over Jenny's mouth and dragged her along the rock ledge to a place where they'd be out of sight. The other men covered their tracks and hid with the horses behind a boulder on the opposite canyon wall.

As the rider came into view, Jenny's quick intake of air let Two Knives know she recognized the rider.

"Who is he?" Two Knives whispered, barely lifting his hand from Jenny's mouth.

"My husband," she answered in an obedient hush. One of the braves who waited in the shadows across from Two Knives and Jenny leveled his rifle to kill David and claim a much needed third horse. Jenny tensed, knowing she couldn't save her husband. She turned pleading brown eyes toward Two Knives. His face remained impassive, but he signaled the brave to let David pass.

David rode through the canyon oblivious to the danger surrounding him. *He seems happy or at least at peace,* Jenny thought. As David passed safely through the canyon and disappeared, Jenny's strength gave out and she fell back against Two Knives. At least for now, David was safe.

Two Knives took his hand from Jenny's mouth and signaled his braves to move out. He carried Jenny down the ledge to the canyon floor and set her down. He looked at her thoughtfully.

Jenny, in turn, studied the man before her. He wasn't as young as she'd thought. His long, straight hair betrayed some gray, and while he was lean and well muscled, his face was etched with lines of experience and age.

"Come," Two Knives commanded, and Jenny walked quickly to keep up with him. The braves moved the horses skillfully down the side of the canyon and onto the rocky floor. They spoke in Apache to Two Knives as they joined him.

From what little Apache Jenny understood, she knew they were questioning him about his decision to let David go free. Two Knives quickly put an end to their questions with an angry scowl. He lifted Jenny onto the back of her horse and leaped up behind her. She was thankful Two Knives didn't re-tie her hands and feet. She knew this was a sign of trust, and she had no desire to betray that confidence.

Once through the canyon, they turned south, picking out the easier trails through the mountainous land. The sun beat down, and while the men seemed not to notice the heat, Jenny grew increasingly weak.

Two Knives sensed Jenny's struggle and signaled his braves to change course. He led the party to a small cave whose entrance was hidden by surrounding vegetation. Two Knives slid down the horse's broad backside and reached up to pull Jenny down. Jenny felt ashamed when her knees buckled, and Two Knives lifted her into his arms. He displayed only disinterested reserve as he entered the cave and placed her on the ground.

The air was cool, and Jenny welcomed the rest. She was confident she wasn't in any real danger. Two Knives could have easily killed her at the mission. With this realization, Jenny crumbled to the floor of the cave and slept.

Several hours later, Two Knives was shaking her awake. Jenny sat up with a start, forgetting where she was. She put the back of her hand to her mouth to stifle a scream. Two Knives seemed unconcerned and handed her a piece of the smoked meat they'd taken from her larder.

"We go now," he said and helped Jenny to her feet.

Jenny nodded and accepted the meat. Her stomach was growling hungrily. She followed Two Knives outside where the horses waited impatiently.

Knowing the matched bays were a docile pair, Jenny was alarmed to find them stomping the ground and snorting at the dust.

"What's wrong with them?" she asked in English only to repeat herself in Spanish.

"They smell the water. Big river is just beyond the pass."

Jenny suddenly realized how far the horses had traveled without receiving much water. She wondered at their ability to continue and thanked God for providing the needed refreshment to keep them strong.

Two Knives lifted Jenny across the horse's back. Instead of mounting in back of her, he led the horse. Night was coming quickly and a missed step could mean the end to a much-needed means of transportation.

Jenny had a great deal of time to think as she clung to the horse's mane. How long would they travel before Two Knives was reunited with his renegade band? Why had they taken her? Would she ever see David again? Woven throughout Jenny's thoughts were the vivid memories of a terrified ten-year-old girl who'd vowed to hate the Indians, especially Apaches.

Brilliant stars filled the moonless night, and Jenny could hear the rushing water of the Rio Grande in the distance. They walked the banks of the Rio Grande until Two Knives stopped to water the horses. Jenny felt them cruel to allow the bays such a small amount, but said nothing as Two

Knives joined her on the horse's back. The bays were spirited and agitated as they were forced to move away from the water.

"Pull up your skirts," Two Knives said to Jenny. He waited for her to obey before edging the bay back to the river.

The remaining braves doubled up on the other bay and followed Two Knives. Jenny gasped at the icy cold as the horse waded in chest high water. Her legs grew numb by the time they reached the opposite bank.

Two Knives helped her down and instructed her to rub her legs with her dry skirt and petticoat. Without hesitation, Jenny sat on a rock and vigorously rubbed her legs until she felt the blood warming them. She was thankful she'd not argued when Two Knives had instructed her to hike up her skirt. Surprised by his thoughtfulness, Jenny contemplated the Indian warrior as he once again allowed the horses to drink from the river.

Three days later, Two Knives was reunited with his people. Jenny was startled to find most of the renegades to be elderly and feeble. She said nothing as Two Knives helped her from the bay and led her to an old man.

"Grandfather," Two Knives said as he

embraced the man. "I have brought you a gift."

Jenny realized she was being given to the old man and tried to appear congenial about the matter.

Two Knives turned to her and spoke in Spanish, "You are to care for my grandfather and his two wives. They are old and cannot gather the wood and food as they could when they were young. I will bring fresh meat and you will prepare it for them. Do this and you will be treated well."

Jenny nodded and moved to stand beside the aged warrior. "I will do this with a glad heart," she answered. Two Knives nodded in appreciation and showed a hint of a smile.

Summer arrived, and Jenny worked hard to help the old man she simply called Grandfather and his aging wives, Wandering Doe and Mescal Blossom. Grandfather had once been an important chief among Water's Edge People, his clan. His wife Mescal Blossom was a medicine woman who taught Jenny many things about using herbs and roots. Wandering Doe was Mescal Blossom's sister. As was often the case, she was wife number two to her older sister's husband.

Jenny kept a watchful eye toward the

horizon, hoping and praying David would come for her, yet she feared if David engaged the cavalry at Santa Fe, the elderly band of renegades would be murdered. Funny, she thought to herself, she didn't hate these people who held her captive.

With each passing day, Jenny also realized she could no longer ignore the changes in her body that pointed to another baby. The Indians were sure to notice her once trim figure was being transformed. It frightened her to think about bearing another child, so she plunged into her duties with new zeal that surprised her as much as it did the aging Apaches.

Jenny had worked hard to learn the Apache language, so when Grandfather stopped her one day as she gathered firewood, she no longer felt the need to struggle with each word.

"You work like one of the people."

Jenny knew he was offering her a compliment.

"Thank you, Grandfather. It pleases me to help you."

"Sit with me," he motioned and eased his body onto the ground.

Jenny quickly joined him but offered no help. It would have disgraced him as a warrior to accept the assistance of a woman, especially a white woman.

"You carry a child," he said matter-of-factly as his white hair, secured by a leather beaded band, blew across his shoulders.

"Yes," Jenny replied softly. She had tried so hard to forget the child she carried, but God wouldn't let it pass so easily from her heart.

"Mescal Blossom told me this when you first arrived," the old man announced. Jenny's mouth dropped open in surprise, but she said nothing. "My wife is very wise about such things. She bore nine children, and Wandering Doe, another five. She is very wise."

Jenny nodded and asked, "Where are your children now, Grandfather?"

"They live on the reservation," he spoke stiffly. "They live as dogs under the white man's table, waiting for the scraps of food the white man throws them."

"Why didn't they stay with you?" Jenny asked curiously.

"Some did for a time. Others were taken away in chains. They did not desire to go, but they had no choice. Many died in great battle. Most of my children walk in the spirit world under the earth."

"Tell me of it, Grandfather," Jenny encouraged, wanting to understand the

Apache way. She was beginning to realize she had the opportunity to witness to these elderly people.

"The underworld has two homes for the spirit people. One is beautiful and green. The people who have performed great deeds and have met the approval of N'de go there. The other is a barren desert where witches torment their souls. One must live a good life and die a good death to avoid that place."

"Have you ever heard of Jesus, Grandfather?" Jenny asked gently.

"The white man's God has great power, but we do not accept His way. I will rest now. You will help the women," the old man said, dismissing her.

Jenny walked away silently. She had a renewed spirit as she realized God had led her to these aging people in order to put her past in order as well as to lead them to an understanding of salvation. Her hand fell to her rounding abdomen as she thought of a way to witness to Grandfather. Who could know the mind of God?

CHAPTER 16

First, David smelled the smoke. Then he saw it billowing to the sky. He urged his gelding to go faster and rounded the canyon wall in time to see brilliant red and orange flames burst through the second-story windows of his home.

"Jenny!" He pushed his nervous horse to the gate and tied him securely before running toward the house. The lance caught his eye immediately. It had been driven into the ground as a calling card of the owner and destroyer of his home. Apache!

"Jenny!" he yelled repeatedly as he frantically searched the grounds. The fear that she was inside the flames drove David to find some sign that would prove otherwise. Nearing the barn, he found it. Two spilt buckets of milk. Completing his search of the yard, David rode hard to Bandelero to call on Daniel's and Lillie's help. His mind couldn't shake the image of his beloved

Jenny being taken captive by those she'd always feared most — Apaches.

Barely taking the time to tether his horse, David burst through the door of Daniel's office. The room was empty.

"Daniel! Lillie! Come quick!" David cried as he moved through the house. Lillie and Daniel met him in the hallway.

"What is it?" Daniel asked.

"It's Jenny," David said frantically. "The Apache burned down our house and took her."

"The Apache? There's no Apache reservation around these parts. Are you sure?" Daniel questioned, taking hold of David's shoulders.

"They left a lance. It was Apache alright. They must be renegades; not all the Indians accepted living on reservations," David declared. "I was just getting back from visiting the Pueblos and found the whole place up in flames. Apparently, Jenny had been milking when they came. I found the buckets of spilt milk in the yard between the house and the barn."

Lillie paled at the thought of Jenny being taken captive. "Dear Lord," she breathed a prayer, "please protect Jenny."

David's distraught face pushed Daniel into action. "We've got to get word to Garrett. If there's a renegade band of Apache, he'll want to protect his own family. Lillie," Daniel said turning to his wife, "you let the sheriff know. I'll ride with David to Piñon Canyon." Lillie nodded in understanding.

"We can take my horses and let yours rest," Daniel said as he pushed David to the door. "Bring your horse around back and we'll stable him and saddle the others." David nodded, grateful Daniel had taken charge.

Within minutes, Daniel and David were off in the direction of Garrett and Maggie Lucas's ranch, Piñon Canyon. Lillie watched as they rode away.

"Dear Lord, please surround them with Your protection," she whispered and went in search of the sheriff.

Maggie Intissar Lucas plucked another of her hair pins from the hands of her two-year-old son and sighed. Putting it back in place, Maggie pulled the boy into her arms.

"Gavin Lucas, why can't you be more like your sister?" the red-headed Maggie asked.

"Baby Doolie!" Gavin said proudly.

Maggie shook her head, "No, not baby Julie; your older sister, Daughtry."

"Dotty," Gavin said, giving it his best.

"That's close enough," Maggie smiled.

"Now, why don't you go be a good boy and stay out of trouble?"

"Because he's good at being a boy," Garrett Lucas said, bounding into the room to take his son. He tossed Gavin high into the air and caught the giggling boy in his arms. "Boys have a harder time staying out of trouble."

"I imagine that is especially true given the fact he's your son," Maggie teased.

A bearded Garrett Lucas let out a laugh as he put Gavin down. Gavin's little legs were already running before his father let his feet touch the floor. In a flash, Gavin was out the door and off to find his sister. Garrett pulled Maggie into his arms and kissed her.

"And what kind of remark is that to make in front of a man's son? If I didn't know better, I'd think you gave birth to another girl on purpose," Garrett laughed.

"Maybe I did," Maggie said, cocking her head to one side. "You always said I was the stubbornest woman you'd ever met."

"Stubborn enough to test the patience of God Himself," Garrett agreed and whirled Maggie in the air.

"Stop it," Maggie chided. "You'll wake up Julie."

Garrett stopped and Maggie melted

against him. How good it was to be Mrs. Garrett Lucas! She felt her heart might burst from the love she felt for this man.

The peaceful moment was broken as five-year-old Daughtry came running in with Gavin close behind. "Mama! Papa! It's Uncle David and Uncle Daniel," she called out breathlessly.

"Here?" Maggie questioned as Daughtry pulled on Garrett's hand.

"Yup," Daughtry replied.

"Yes," Maggie corrected.

"Yes," Daughtry repeated the word. "They're riding real fast too."

"Something must be wrong," Maggie said, looking with concern at her husband.

"I'll see what the problem is. You keep the children here," Garrett instructed, and Maggie turned to see if the baby was still sleeping. The soft, downy-headed Julie slept soundly.

Maggie took Gavin in hand, and Daughtry wrapped herself around her mother's skirts. Maggie's heart beat faster at the sound of raised voices in the yard. What could have happened that would bring both Daniel and David to Piñon Canyon in the middle of the day?

The three men came into the house and the look on Garrett's face told Maggie the news wasn't good. "You children go to the playroom and wait for me there," Maggie instructed.

"No!" Gavin protested, but followed his sister at the sight of his father's frown.

When the children were out of earshot, Maggie turned to the grim-faced men. "What is it?"

"Jenny's been taken by Apaches," Garrett said.

Maggie's face paled.

"How? When?" she questioned, plunging her hands deep into her apron pockets.

"This morning. I'd been out at the Pueblo village for several days, and when I came back this morning, the entire place was on fire," David blurted out. Daniel put a hand on his shoulder.

"Are you sure they took her? She wasn't in the . . . in the . . ." Maggie couldn't finish the question.

"No, I'm sure she wasn't in the house. They surprised her outside. They must have come upon her while she was doing the chores," David replied.

"What about the children?" Garrett asked.

"The Pueblo had already come to take them back to the village. An epidemic took the lives of so many children the elders insisted the orphans return to their people."

"That must have devastated Jenny," Maggie commented.

"It did," David said softly. "But that's an entirely different subject. We have to go after her. That's why I'm here."

"The first order of business is to secure the ranch and get Maggie and the kids to town," Garrett stated.

"They can stay with Lillie and the boys," Daniel offered.

Garrett nodded. "Thanks, friend."

"But I don't want to leave the ranch," Maggie protested.

"We don't know what dangers lurk in the area," Garrett said as he tried to soothe Maggie. "I don't think they'll still be in the area, but Bandelero will be safer. Besides, I'll feel a heap better knowing you and the children are safe while I'm gone."

"Gone?" Maggie asked fearfully. "Where are you going?"

"I'm going with David and Daniel to find Jenny." Garrett's words hit hard. Maggie blinked back tears. "It's going to be alright, Maggie. God will watch over you and Lillie. You'll be fine."

"It's not me I'm worried about," Maggie said, her voice cracking. "I know you need to do this, but I wish none of you were going. Now, if you'll excuse me," she stated

195

with renewed resolve, "I'll get the children's things together."

Garrett touched her cheek, and Maggie paused long enough to look into his eyes. "Dear God," she silently prayed, "please bring him back to me. Bring them all back safely."

When Maggie was gone, Garrett turned his attention to David and Daniel. "I'll check with the ranch hands and see if anyone wants to ride with us. Then we'll send someone to Santa Fe to notify the cavalry."

"The cavalry!" David exclaimed. "That'll take days."

Garrett glanced at Daniel and then offered David an apologetic look. "I'm sorry, Buddy. You have to face facts. Finding Jenny may take weeks, even months."

"Months?" David and Daniel questioned at once.

"There haven't been any Apache around here since the roundup of '86. The soldiers moved them west of the Rio Grande to the reservation. These have to be renegades, and they aren't going to stay in the near vicinity. At least, that's what I'm banking on. We're going to pack plenty of provisions and plan to be out for weeks, possibly longer."

"I can't believe it," David said and sank to

a chair with his head in his hands. "I can't ask you two to go with me. I can't take you away from your families for that long. I thought maybe a few days, a week at the most. I didn't consider the danger. I can't ask you to do this."

"You didn't ask," Garrett stated firmly. "Now let's get moving. The longer we take, the colder the trail."

Within an hour, Garrett had rounded up five men to accompany them in the search for Jenny Monroe. Their first step was to evacuate Maggie and the children to Bandelero. For greater safety, Garrett had Maggie and the children ride in the bed of the wagon, which he drove. The other men surrounded the wagon on horseback, their Winchester lever action rifles ready for a fight.

The trip from Piñon Canyon, although tense, passed uneventfully. At Bandelero, Garrett traded the wagon in for his horse and rechecked the supplies.

Maggie held fast to Lillie's hand. They'd been best friends nearly all their lives. Lillie alone could understand the apprehension in Maggie's heart. Silently, they stood and shared each other's fears and hopes.

Garrett motioned for his men to join in as David led them in prayer. The men took off their hats and bowed their heads as David spoke.

"Father, we ask for Your help in finding Jenny. Please guide us and protect my friends from danger. Lord, I ask that You go to wherever Jenny is and surround her with Your angels. Keep her safe and let her feel confident we're coming for her. In Jesus' Name. Amen."

"Mount up," Garrett called out. He turned to take Maggie in his arms. "I've told the children to be good and to remember their prayers. I guess the same thing holds true for you," he said with a grin.

"Please be careful," Maggie said, unable to smile at Garrett's humor. "I can't bear to think of you being gone for so long. Please hurry home." She sobbed the words despite her resolve to be strong. Garrett held her closely, breathing in the scent of her cologne.

"Please be careful," Lillie echoed her friend's words. "Oh Daniel, I love you so. Please, please come home safe to the boys and me."

Daniel reached up and held Lillie's face in his hands. "I'll come home soon. You'll see. Just remember to pray for us and take good care of the children." He lowered his lips and kissed her gently.

Reluctantly, the women let go of their husbands. They clung to each other as they watched Garrett and Daniel mount their horses. Long after the dust of the horses had obscured any possible view of their husbands, Maggie and Lillie waved good-bye. Then they fell into each other's arms and cried. They cried for each other and they cried for themselves. Mostly, they cried for Jenny, knowing they might never see her again.

CHAPTER 17

As the summer months brought uncomfortable heat, Jenny's body filled out in a way that left no one questioning her condition. She'd begun to feel movement, although she denied to herself that a baby was the reason for such activity. Instead, Jenny worked harder to insure the elderly Apache people had food to eat and warm blankets in store for winter. She also spent more time trying to witness to Grandfather.

Grandfather's stoic silence first led Jenny to believe he had little or no interest in her beliefs. Yet as the summer wore on, Jenny found Grandfather asking more questions. He wasn't averse to adding another god to his collection of worshipped spirits, but he saw no reason to leave his own beliefs behind. Jenny prayed God would guide her to say the right things, but she knew while she planted spiritual seeds, God was the gardener.

Two Knives appeared occasionally to bring a deer or antelope for Mescal Blossom. Jenny learned Mescal Blossom was Two Knives's mother-in-law. While her daughter had died several years earlier, Mescal Blossom was still esteemed.

In Apache families, the mother-in-law was given the honor of accepting the game and deciding who in the family would receive a portion. With Mescal Blossom's hands growing more and more twisted from age, she appointed Jenny to care for the kill.

Late one afternoon, Jenny was sitting on the ground scraping hair from a wet deer hide when Two Knives approached with an armload of brush for firewood.

"Two Knives, gathering firewood is a woman's job. You needn't dishonor yourself as a warrior by gathering brush," Jenny protested as she looked up from her work.

Two Knives placed the wood beside the wickiup and nodded slightly. "The only dishonor comes in allowing the old and weak to suffer when I am strong and capable of helping them. The old ways are good ones if you live in a tribal family with many warriors and women. Here, the old and dying cannot work as they could when they were young. We will work for them." He walked away without waiting for Jenny to reply.

Jenny thought his words quite sensible and resolved never again to question Two Knives when he performed extra tasks. Turning back to her work, she continued to scrape the hair from the hide and didn't hear Grandfather sit behind her in the doorway of the wickiup.

She began pounding out the rougher spots on the hide and thought of verses in the Bible that spoke of making the rough places smooth. Absorbed in these thoughts, Jenny was startled by Grandfather's voice.

"When my people were many, before the white man forced them to the reservation, I would tell many stories; histories of N'de and the Sun Spirit. The children would gather round me and listen with reverence while I told of the animal spirits and why we ask the hunted to forgive the hunter."

"And why was that, Grandfather?" Jenny questioned.

"It is only right to ask the animal to forgive us. We do not take its life because we are angry or seeking revenge. No, we kill the animal for our food and clothes. This he does not mind, so he forgives us. Apache believe all things have spirit. One-From-Whom-All-Things-Come gave all things to N'de to take and use."

"Is that why your people raid?" Jenny asked.

Grandfather looked out across the desert and up into the sky. "If the Great Spirit has given us all things, N'de have only to use as they need."

"But you took me captive. I'm not a thing. I am a human being and a child of God," Jenny said bravely.

"You are not a human being. You are not N'de," Grandfather answered flatly.

"Grandfather, I have listened to N'de ways," Jenny interjected, "and I've been a good captive."

"You speak the truth," Grandfather admitted.

"I know N'de have their beliefs, but I have mine too. I believe in one God. My heavenly Father is God over all. He sent His Son, Jesus Christ, to save all people, not just N'de, but all people from their sins."

"I do not know this word 'sins'," the old man replied.

Jenny prayed for the right words. "Sins are the things we do that we know are wrong. Things that go against God's law. Jesus came to this world so we might be forgiven for those sins."

"Forgiven?" Grandfather questioned.

"N'de ask the animals to forgive them

before the N'de kill them, but the N'de really need to ask God to forgive them before they lose their own lives. Forgiveness is when those sins are canceled. They are not accepted as right, but they are forgotten."

"This is not the way of N'de. When white man does wrong to Apache, we do not forgive. It is not our way."

"I know," Jenny said softly. "But Grandfather, if you do not accept God's gift of forgiveness and forgive those who've wronged you, you cannot see God."

"I am an old man. It is not easy to accept new ways, but I know your spirit is sweet. Do you believe this forgiveness is possible for N'de?"

"Of course, I do. What you don't know about me, Grandfather, is my family was killed by N'de." Jenny waited for a response, but the only sign of Grandfather having heard her was the slight nod of his head. Jenny drew a deep breath and continued. "I was a small child, and an Apache raiding party attacked our wagon train at dawn and killed almost everyone."

"It was our people's way," Grandfather said.

Jenny got the distinct impression it was his way of apologizing.

"I understand that, Grandfather. What I'm

trying to explain is I forgive the Apache for killing my family and I will not seek revenge for them." Jenny suddenly realized her words were true. For so many years she'd wondered if forgiving the Apache was possible.

"You have a good heart," the old man said as he considered Jenny's words. "You have been good to the Apache, and I believe your words are true."

"Grandfather, as much as you believe this a good thing that I do, God has done a much greater thing for all mankind. God sent His only Son to die so we might live in heaven with Him. When we ask God to forgive us, He does. He doesn't seek revenge for our mistakes. Instead He offers us life in heaven."

"I will consider your words," Grandfather said as he struggled to his feet.

"Thank you, Grandfather." Jenny watched the old man walk away. She was elated. The old man had never given such a positive response to her words of salvation and God's forgiveness.

"Thank You, Father," Jenny prayed. "Thank You for allowing me to help these people." The baby moved sharply within her and Jenny changed the focus of her prayer. "Lord, please help me to feel good about this baby. I'm so afraid to go through this again. I know I prayed for a baby of my own, but now I'm afraid. Here I am separated from my husband, living with the Apache, and carrying a child. Please help me to feel Your peace and not worry about the outcome." Jenny looked heavenward and noticed the sky was filling with heavy black clouds. Forgetting herself, she quickly went to work to finish staking out the hide before it rained.

The storm hit sometime in the night, causing Jenny to bolt upright at the crack of thunder. Through the dim glow of the dying fire, she could make out Grandfather's sleeping form on the opposite side of the wickiup. Pulling her knees to her chest, she sighed. The thunder boomed again and the rain poured until Jenny feared the wickiup would flood.

Beside her, Mescal Blossom and Wandering Doe snored loudly, not noticing the storm. Jenny wished it were that easy for her. Her mind filled with concern for David. Where was he? Was he out in the storm suffering because of her?

Jenny laid back on the woven blanket and thought of her husband. What would he think when he found her and learned of their baby? Would he be happy or would it be cause for grief? Thoughts of David's distress haunted her as Jenny drifted off to sleep. Eventually, the noise of the storm faded, leaving only the steady patter of falling rain.

The next morning when Jenny awoke, the ground had dried. Jenny dressed quickly in a loose doeskin dress, which Mescal Blossom had helped her make. The soft leather felt good against her skin, and Jenny couldn't deny that the style was far more comfortable than the dresses she was used to.

Emerging from the wickiup, Jenny noticed Mescal Blossom was busy using a bone awl to punch holes in thick pieces of undressed skins. Jenny watched in fascination as the old woman's gnarled hands labored at the task with relative ease.

"Some days," Mescal Blossom said, never stopping to look up at Jenny, "the Great Spirit gives me strength in my hands. I never want him to think me ungrateful, so I work hard to prove I am worthy."

Jenny nodded and squatted down beside her. "What are you making?"

"I make good boots for your feet. See how toes of boot turn up to face the sky?" Mescal Blossom questioned, showing Jenny her own moccasined feet. Jenny nodded. "Comanche call N'de *Ta'-ashi*. It means *Turned up*." The old woman smiled slightly as if it were some great joke among the N'de.

Jenny was touched that Mescal Blossom was spending her rare agility to make her a gift. "Why do you make boots for me, Mescal Blossom? You should make them for Grandfather," Jenny suggested.

"Grandfather told me to make these boots for your journey," Mescal Blossom answered frankly.

"What journey?" Jenny questioned, but the old woman simply shrugged her shoulders and went back to work. Jenny's curiosity was piqued, so she went in search of Grandfather.

She found him sitting on top of a small mound of dirt, isolated and away from the rest of the clan. He looked to be praying or meditating on something, so Jenny decided to walk back to the wickiups and continue her own tasks. Grandfather, however, held out his hand and beckoned her to join him.

"I didn't mean to disturb you, Grandfather," Jenny said as she sat down on the ground near the old man.

"You did not disturb me. I wanted to talk to you about the one God." Grandfather's words caused Jenny to forget what she'd come to ask him about.

"What did you want to discuss?"

"N'de ways are dying, and white man's ways are all around. My people cannot live another winter in the cold, so I must move them to the reservation."

"I think it would be best," Jenny admitted.

"It will always be a matter of sight," Grandfather replied. "White man sees new land for many more white men. He does not see that N'de already live here. He tells us to go and we go, but he cannot see that the land still does not belong to him. Land and all that exists belongs to One-From-Whom-All-Things-Come. I am a tired old man, and I am nearly ready to die. I have thought on your words of the one God and believe your spirit speaks truth. N'de killed your people, yet you serve me with a glad heart. Your God has allowed you to find stillness inside. I want to accept this forgiveness and return with my people to our families on the reservation where we might live our final days in stillness."

Jenny was uncertain whether Grandfather was willing to forsake his Apache religion, but she decided it was for God to deal with Grandfather's heart. "I am glad, Grandfather, and I know God is happy too."

Grandfather nodded and listened as Jenny

continued to share the message of salvation with him. After praying with Grandfather and listening to him accept Jesus Christ as his Savior, Jenny felt an exhilaration and exhaustion she'd never known. For the first time since becoming a servant to the Apache, she believed her captivity provided nothing more than a mission field that she'd been prepared for since childhood.

CHAPTER 18

The next morning, Grandfather met with his people to discuss the move to the reservation. Jenny wasn't allowed to join the circle of N'de, but she could easily overhear the words exchanged.

Two Knives and the other young men were against moving, while the older ones were weary and ready to consider Grandfather's suggestion. Jenny heard Grandfather explain that his family would join with those Apache at the reservation, and if any others desired, they could travel with him. Either way, a move would be required for the entire clan as fall was nearly upon them and the game in the area was exhausted. It was suddenly clear to Jenny why Mescal Blossom had worked constantly to finish the boots.

By nightfall, all but four of the N'de had agreed to accompany Grandfather to the reservation. Two Knives and three of his friends agreed to move west into unsettled land where they could remain free.

Grandfather approached Jenny after the exhausting ordeal. He sat down beside her and watched silently as she ground corn. After nearly fifteen minutes of silence, he finally spoke.

"I was wrong to say you were not a human being. You have worked as one of the Apache since Two Knives brought you to me. I cannot force a human being to remain against his will. I will let you go."

Jenny's mouth dropped open in surprise. Funny, she thought, she'd never once questioned what might become of her after Grandfather joined up with his people on the reservation.

"I can go home?" she questioned.

"Yes," the old man smiled. He signaled Mescal Blossom to bring the boots. "These are for your journey. You have many miles to go. I will give you one of the horses, but you will still have to walk. Mescal Blossom's boots will make your way easier."

Jenny took the knee-high boots and smiled appreciatively. "Thank you, both. I will wear them and remember my N'de friends," she said as she cast aside her well-worn shoes and slipped on the boots. "They fit perfectly!" Jenny exclaimed as she got to her feet. "Now I really look N'de."

Grandfather laughed, and Mescal Blossom nodded in agreement. "You will leave tomorrow morning. Two of my braves will go with you as far as the big river. From there the trail will be easier, and you will be able to find your way."

"But I know nothing of the trails, Grandfather," Jenny protested. "Can't they take me closer to home — at least as far as the Pueblo village?"

"No, the risk would be too great. Your people will be looking for you even after these many moons. It would not be safe for my braves. You told me God is great and powerful. He will take you on your way when the braves leave you."

Jenny nodded. Grandfather was right. She wasn't giving God credit for her freedom or for the fact He would guard her on her journey home. "God will protect me, Grandfather. My Father in heaven will lead me home."

The following morning before the sun was up, Grandfather gave his braves final instructions. Jenny was carefully put on one of the bays. She had no choice but to ride straddled, fearing that without a saddle she'd fall from the horse and lose her baby.

She hugged Mescal Blossom and Wandering Doe as she carefully leaned down from the horse. In the distance she saw Two Knives and felt disappointed he wouldn't be the one to take her back. She waved good-bye to him and then to Grandfather.

"I won't forget you, Grandfather. You helped my heart heal. I will pray for your safety on the way to the reservation and that your people will be strong and live long enough for you to share the truth of God with them."

"I will tell my people of the God who forgives their sin and of His Son Jesus who gave His blood."

"I'll miss you and your people," Jenny said honestly. She was anxious to be with her husband and friends, but she regretted she would never again see the old man and his people.

The sun was just peeking over the horizon when Mescal Blossom brought Grandfather a handful of pollen. As was their Apache way, Grandfather faced east and blew the pollen toward the sun. "I will ask for a blessing," Grandfather said, "not from the sun which warms our land, but from the Great God's Son who sent you to N'de." Jenny smiled and nodded.

They were on their way before the sun was fully risen. Jenny was uncomfortable riding the huge bay but said nothing. Her Apache escort ran on foot beside her, so it would seem ungrateful to complain. Jenny had learned long ago the Apache walked almost everywhere they went. Apache men could often travel fifty miles on foot in a single day. Their loping run didn't wind them.

As she rode, Jenny allowed herself to think of David, a luxury she'd not often indulged in. The fear of never seeing her husband again had been too painful, so Jenny had concentrated on the matters at hand. Now, however, she was going home — home to David.

Would he have changed much? Jenny worried David would have spent every waking moment in worry and grief over her. She could imagine his heartache at finding his home destroyed and his wife missing. Then a panicked thought struck her. What if David thought she'd burned in the fire?

"Oh God," she whispered, "please don't let David give up. Please let him know I'm alright, Lord. Don't let him believe me dead."

David bolted upright. "Jenny!" he cried, bringing his closest companions awake.

"What is it?" Garrett asked as he got up and wiped the sleep from his eyes.

"Yeah," Daniel added with a yawn, "what's all the noise about?"

"I just felt, I mean . . ." David shook his head as if to clear the sleep from his mind. "I can't explain it, but I thought I heard Jenny."

Garrett smiled sadly. "Don't worry, David. We'll find her." Daniel nodded and stretched.

"I know we will," David spoke confidently. "I can't explain why, call it the peace of God or whatever, but I feel more positive about this than ever before. I know she's alright, and I know we'll find her very soon."

Daniel seemed to catch his brother's enthusiasm. "We best get crackin' then. The sun's already up, and we're wasting time."

Garrett nodded in agreement. "From the looks of it," he added, "the boys already have the coffee made and the other horses ready. We must be getting too old for this."

"I'll say," Daniel said as he tied up his bedroll. "I'm still not used to sleeping on the ground." Garrett and David both laughed at this, knowing Daniel had lived a more pampered life. "Besides," Daniel added, "I'm a heap older than you two."

"He's got us there, Garrett," David said as he picked up his saddle and started to walk away. "Maybe we should start calling him Gramps." David ignored Daniel's bedroll as it struck him in the back. His heart was lighter than it had been in months.

Three days out on the trail, Jenny's ears caught the roar of the Rio Grande. Apprehension filled her heart as she realized her companions would be returning to the Apache.

The Apache men, who'd hardly spoken a dozen words the entire trip, gave Jenny explicit directions for getting home. Jenny accepted the reins the men had alternately led the horse by. She thanked them for their help and followed their directions to a shallow crossing of the Rio Grande.

The bay picked his way through the icy waters while Jenny concentrated on staying seated. The bay's right shoulder dropped, then the left as he made his way across the uneven river bottom. Jenny was grateful not to have her long gown to worry about. The fringed bottom of the Apache dress she wore resisted the water, as did the knee-high moccasin boots.

After only minutes, Jenny landed safely on the opposite bank of the Rio Grande. She turned to wave to her traveling companions, only to discover they had disappeared. Feeling isolated, Jenny whispered a prayer before heading the bay toward home.

"Father," she said softly, "I'm in Your hands completely. You know I can't get on and off this horse without help, so I pray You will deliver me into the hands of those who love me." Jenny looked out across the dry, sandy land. The sage had faded to a dusty green, and the small clumps of grass were dried brown.

By the position of the sun, Jenny could tell it was very early, so she pushed the bay to cover as much land as they could before nightfall. The day passed in a blur of scenery that Jenny compared to landmarks in the directions she'd been given. She had passed Two Fingers Rock and the path where the crooked trees grew. She put the white canyon behind her where volcanic rock had formed chalky white walls with narrow passageways. An icy chill caused her to shiver as the wind came down from the mountains.

Mescal Blossom had given Jenny two warm Indian blankets before she'd departed the company of the N'de. One she used as a cushion between herself and the horse's bristly backside. The other she hugged close in order to keep warm.

The horse, ever faithful, trudged on. He bore up well under Jenny's slight weight, but the strain of the climb into the mountains caused him to breathe heavier. Jenny considered dismounting, but she worried because she had never dismounted a horse without the security of a stirrup. With her rounded abdomen, Jenny feared she might harm the baby if she fell in her efforts to get off the horse.

As if recognizing Jenny's thoughts, the baby moved sharply, causing Jenny to gasp. She'd tried not to think about the child she carried, but she knew God wanted her to take joy and hope in this baby.

Just then the horse whinnied, sensing something up ahead. Jenny braced herself, wondering what she should do. Obviously, the horse sensed something she couldn't see.

The horse began to prance nervously, and Jenny concentrated all her efforts on staying seated. Whatever lay ahead was making the horse anxious, and that only caused Jenny to think she should be concerned, too. She managed to slide off the bay. Holding tightly to the horse's reins, Jenny waited and listened. The rustling of the wind in the lodgepole pines caused the horse to whinny.

Jenny tried to lead the bay forward, but he refused. She decided to wait for a few moments in hopes that whatever was spooking the horse would pass.

Suddenly, voices could be heard, and Jenny's heart pounded harder. She strained to hear what was being said. Was it Indian or English? Horses could also be heard, and Jenny knew then what the bay had been reacting to.

She started to push the horse toward a thicket of trees and brush, but something caught her attention. She remained perfectly still, hoping to hear better. Then it came to her. The voices were louder and clearer, speaking not only the English she'd longed to hear, but in voices that she recognized. David!

Jenny pulled the bay with renewed strength and ran in the direction of the voices. "David!" she called out. "David, it's me Jenny!"

The group of travel-worn men rounded the bend in disbelief. David threw the reins of his horse to Daniel as he flew out of the saddle toward his wife. He didn't notice anything but her face. It was Jenny! At long last he'd found her!

"David," she sobbed and fell into his arms.

"It's you, it's really you!" David exclaimed as he covered Jenny's dirt smudged face with kisses. Suddenly, he stopped and put Jenny at arm's length. "Dear Lord," he whispered as he realized she was pregnant.

Garrett and Daniel interrupted David and took turns hugging Jenny. "Thank God we found you, or was it the other way around?" Garrett asked as he gave Jenny a hearty embrace. "And just look at you. You wear those Apache clothes well. I almost mistook you for an Indian."

Daniel laughed and gave his sister-in-law a quick appraisal before hugging her. "Why didn't you tell us about the baby? We'd have never let you go off gallivanting."

The men didn't notice David moved away several steps, but Jenny did. She tried not to react, but she was hurt that he seemed put off. Did he think her baby was Apache? Surely he'd be wise enough to realize from her size this baby was without a doubt his.

"David?" Garrett questioned as he finally noticed the look on his friend's face.

David looked up but said nothing. How could he explain to them the fear he felt? After the weeks they had spent on the trail looking for his wife, David knew his behavior was not only questionable, it was uncalled for.

"You look like you just swallowed bad water," Garrett said as he stepped over to where David stood. "Are you alright?"

Jenny watched her husband, trying desperately to figure out what he was thinking.

"David?" she questioned as she came forward. "What is it?" She reached out to touch him, but found David's face expressionless.

"We'd best make camp," he said and walked away, leaving Jenny, Daniel, and Garrett to stare dumfounded after him.

CHAPTER 19

"Well, you don't look any worse for wear," Maggie said as she finished frosting the chocolate cake they would eat for supper.

"I feel great," Jenny admitted. "I hope you know how grateful I am to you and Garrett for taking in David and me. I couldn't believe the mess left over at our place."

"You have to remember the first few months were spent looking for you. It was so hard waiting, wondering," Maggie said as she put the knife down and came over to where Jenny was sitting. "I have to admit, it wasn't only my fear for you, but for the men as well. I guess that sounds selfish."

"Not at all," Jenny said and shifted her weight uncomfortably in the chair. "The only way I maintained my sanity was to put my thoughts of David and my loved ones far from the reality of what was happening. I feared I might endanger myself if I didn't cooperate, and to do that required concentrating on my duties."

"I can only imagine," Maggie replied with a shudder. "I guess what's important is you're safe and you're going to have a baby. I'm so excited for you."

"I just wish David was as excited as everybody else is," Jenny said sadly. "I know he's worried. I was too, but now I believe God has answered all my prayers. See, Maggie," Jenny began, "I never realized the hostility toward the Apache that I held on to after all these years. I can't imagine how hateful I would've become if I'd continued to hold on to it."

"God has a way of making us face our bitterness and deal with it," Maggie admitted.

"Yes, he does," Jenny agreed. "I'm afraid that's what David is going through right now. I never saw it before, but I'm beginning to think perhaps David has held resentment toward God for the death of our children. It seems like I've been blind to something I could've helped David with a long time ago."

"Don't be too hard on yourself, Jenny. God brings each of us around in due time. It's His plan, not ours." Maggie's words were just what Jenny needed to hear.

"I'll pray on it," Jenny said as she struggled to her feet. "I'll pray on it and trust God to help David heal."

Maggie nodded and went back to her cake, while Jenny went in search of her husband.

David was sitting alone in the library. Jenny watched him for several minutes before going to stand beside him. It wasn't like David to sit and do nothing. Jenny knew he was troubled and prayed she could offer him some relief from his fears.

"May I join you?" Jenny asked, placing her hand lightly upon David's shoulder.

"Suit yourself," David said indifferently.

Jenny took a seat on the brocade chair opposite David. "I've missed you," she whispered.

"I know," David replied. "I'm sorry, Jenny."

"I want you to know I understand," Jenny said as she studied her husband.

"I'm glad you do, because understanding eludes me," David said flatly.

"I'm not going to press you in this matter, but we've been together for a long time. I remember how patient you were with me while I came to terms with my hatred of the Indians." Jenny hoped David would say something. When he didn't, she continued. "What you don't know is I never really dealt with it until my stay with the Apache."

David suddenly showed a bit of interest.

"I thought I had," Jenny said as she reflected on the matter. "I was certain I had laid the ghosts of my dead family to rest, at least until the day I came out of the barn to find the Apache in my front yard. I never recognized the anger and bitterness until then."

"And?" David asked, wondering what her point was.

"Something happened inside of me, David. I realized I still blamed God for so much of my heartache. The children, our babies, Natty, the raid — you name it, I blamed God for all of it. Here I was the wife of a pastor, ministering God's love to all who would listen, and I still didn't truly believe in it."

David looked away uncomfortably. Jenny got to her feet and walked toward the door.

"I love you, David. Never forget that. Never doubt that my love binds me to you and because of it, we can never truly be separated." Jenny recited the words David had shared with her the night he'd rescued her from Natty Morgan. Jenny's words lingered in the air, long after she had left the room.

David knew Jenny was right. He was harboring anger toward God. But it was impossible for him to deal with it, and listening to Jenny talk about it only made him feel worse. Perhaps that was why he had distanced himself from her. Worst of all, for the first time since deciding to become a minister, David couldn't talk to God.

"I hate the way he sits there and mopes," Maggie said as Garrett finished harnessing the horses to the wagon.

"I do too," he answered and came to put his arm around Maggie. She was holding six-month-old Julie, who was just learning how to pull at her mother's hair.

Garrett pulled off his glove and reached out a finger to his daughter. Julie grabbed on and pulled her father's finger toward her mouth.

"Oh no, you don't," Garrett said as he took his hand away. Julie started to fuss, and Maggie soothed her gently.

"I think she's hungry again," Maggie said and started for the house. Garrett walked with her to get the door and both were surprised when David met them in the doorway.

"I was just coming to get you, Friend," Garrett said as he approached David. "I'm going over to Bandelero, and there's something there I want to show you."

"I don't know, Garrett. I don't much feel like seeing a lot of people."

"Then we won't," Garrett said, leaning over to kiss Maggie good-bye. "I'll be back around supper," he said and turned to David. "Come on. It'll do you good to get out. Maggie will let Jenny know where you are."

"Sure I will, David. You go on with Garrett and I'll whip up a batch of your favorite flan for supper," Maggie said, remembering David's love of Mexican custard.

David finally relented and followed Garrett to the wagon. "I don't know that this is a good idea," he said as he climbed up onto the wagon seat.

"Of course it is," Garrett replied and flicked the reins to put the horses in motion. "I've got quite a proposition for you," he added, but refused to elaborate.

David passed the trip to Bandelero in silence. Garrett, respecting his friend's suffering, chose to spend the time in prayer. He knew it wouldn't be easy to convince David of the positive aspects of his proposal, and he prayed God would show him the best way to deal with his troubled friend.

They stopped first on the south side of town and waited long enough for Daniel to join them. David raised a questioning glance toward Garrett but said nothing. He paid little attention to the conversation Garrett and Daniel shared, nor to the direction in which they were headed. When Garrett brought the wagon to a stop, David lifted his head to find a nearly completed church building.

"Well," Garrett said as he jumped down from the wagon, "what do you think?"

David looked first at Garrett, then to his brother.

"Think of what?" he asked.

"What do you think of your new church?" Daniel said and joined Garrett on the ground. "We thought about it, then we prayed about it, and finally we did something about it. This church is the result."

David shook his head in confusion. "I don't understand what this has to do with me."

"The town needs a parson," Garrett said matter-of-factly. "I had to wonder if maybe God wasn't leading you in a new direction what with the fact that the mission has been burned and there aren't any orphans, at least not at the present."

"So you just listened to God telling you what was best for me? Is that it?" David asked, allowing more anger into his voice than he'd intended.

"Well, little brother, I'd sure guess you weren't doing a heap of listening to Him, yourself. Now I'm not trying to act like I've got a monopoly on God's ear, but I've felt called to help in this project as well. And, I might add, with you in mind."

"I see," David said, trying to control his voice.

"Why don't you come on inside and give it a look over. It seems the least you can do after I drove you out all this way," Garrett said with a grin. "I think you might even like it."

David shrugged and reluctantly joined Garrett and Daniel on the ground. "Alright, show me your church."

Garrett led the way and pushed open the door to the new building. "I figure, we get a couple coats of whitewash on the outside," he said as he entered the building. "Maggie and Lillie want a bell in the tower so people know when it's time to come to church, and I told them we'd think about it."

"You know how they are," Daniel said, picking up the conversation. "They'd have curtains at the windows and pillows on the pews if you gave them a free hand."

David was amazed at the work Garrett and Daniel had gone to on his behalf. "I don't know why you went to all this trouble," he muttered as he inspected a solid oak pulpit at the front of the church.

"You need a congregation, and we need a church. I figured the two went together. I don't expect you to take this on without praying about it," Garrett said. "I just think it might offer you the most ideal solution to your problems."

"And," Daniel interjected as he came to stand beside his brother, "it won't be much longer before your baby will be here. I want you and Jenny to move in with Lillie and me as soon as possible. I'm going to keep a good eye on that wife of yours and bring your baby into the world safe and sound. I'm getting pretty good at it, if I do say so myself."

Garrett laughed. "I'll say."

David tried to smile, but fear gripped his heart. They didn't understand. They hadn't gone through the things he had. They couldn't know what it was like to face the possibility of losing another child.

"Mr. Lucas," a voice called from the front door, "could I have a word with you?" A tall, well-dressed man whom Garrett recognized as the owner of Bandelero's only bank waited at the door for Garrett's answer.

"If you two will excuse me a moment,"

Garrett said and went to see what the man needed.

Daniel took the opportunity to speak to David. He motioned him to take a seat. "I know what you're thinking. I can see it in your eyes. I had the same look in mine when I found out Lillie was pregnant. All I could think about was Katie. Of course, all Lillie could think about was the baby she'd lost in the carriage accident that took her first husband's life."

David nodded, but tightness in his throat wouldn't allow him to speak.

Daniel took a seat beside his brother and continued, "I never wanted to love another woman after Katie died. I never wanted to deal with God again, either. I was such a new Christian, and I didn't have the strength to get through my anguish. I hated myself for turning you away, and I hated God for taking my wife, or at least I thought I did. I couldn't understand why God would allow such a thing to happen, but now that He's sent me Lillie and the boys, I can't imagine life any other way."

"I don't think I can bear it," David finally spoke.

"I know," Daniel answered. "I never thought I could either. But no matter how far you run, you can never outrun God. I know you're trying to outrun Him right now, but it won't work. We both know it."

"It's hard to trust, and I was wrong to ever make an issue of it with you when Katie died," David said sadly.

"No, you weren't. You were telling me what I needed to hear — what God wanted me to hear. I hope I'm returning the favor. Jenny is feeling pretty alone right now. I know, because she cried in my arms and told me so."

David's head snapped up. The thought of his wife seeking comfort from another man unnerved him. "I guess I haven't been what she's needed."

"No, you haven't," Daniel said firmly. "I can still remember the look on your face the day we found her. But more than that, I'll never forget the look on hers. The pain and alienation was enough to make me want to throttle you."

"I didn't mean to hurt her. I don't want to hurt her. I'm just so afraid, and that seems so unmanly. What if this baby dies too?" David questioned with tears in his eyes. "I don't think either one of us could live through the agony. What if Jenny dies during the birthing? All these questions keep going through my mind, and I don't understand why God can't see my pain."

"He does see it," Daniel said as he put his arm around David. "He's never left you, David — you stopped trusting Him to take care of the situation. Like you told me once, you've got to trust Him. It won't be easy, but it's the only way you'll have any peace."

David nodded. "I know you're right." He looked up toward the front of the church. A wooden cross had been erected behind the pulpit — a reminder to him the answer had been given long ago. "I'd like a few minutes alone."

Daniel nodded, gripped David's shoulder, and left.

"Father," David began as he got down on his knees and looked up to the cross, "forgive me for doubting Your wisdom in this situation. Forgive me, too, for the anger I've held inside all these years. Like Jenny, I didn't realize the way I'd allowed resentment to root itself in my heart. I think back to the children Jenny bore, and it hurts so much to remember their passing. I know they're safely in heaven with You, but God," David broke down and cried, "I miss them so, and I miss the way Jenny used to be before she lost them." Moments of silence passed as David cried before God.

When David was spent, peace filled his soul. God had filled his emptiness. David got to his feet and wiped his face.

He came out from the church and found Daniel and Garrett waiting for his decision. They stood talking at the wagon but fell silent as he approached.

"I'll pastor your church until you get someone who's better suited. I'm still not convinced my ministry isn't with the Indian people, but I'll pray about it and do as God directs me."

Garrett grinned and Daniel nodded.

"Now," David said as he climbed up on the wagon seat, "I'd like to get home to my wife."

CHAPTER 20

With little ceremony, Jenny and David were settled into Lillie and Daniel's house in Bandelero. For the first time since coming home from her stay with the Apaches, Jenny felt all was well. David's faith had been restored, and with it, Jenny's strength. She'd never realized how much she looked to David for her courage.

Jenny looked out the window and down the street where a distinct hammering could be heard. She knew David and Garrett were working feverishly before the onset of winter to build a small parsonage. God had truly provided for all their needs, Jenny realized. Patting her oversized abdomen, she thanked God for meeting the desires of her heart, as well.

She sat down uncomfortably and waited for the tightening to pass. Her labor had started an hour earlier, but Jenny didn't want to worry David with a lengthy wait, so she had said nothing to him when he left to work on the house.

The pains were coming closer together, however, and Jenny knew she needed to let Daniel and Lillie know so they could prepare for her delivery. Gingerly making her way down the hall, Jenny found Daniel in his office. She grinned when Daniel looked up from his supply ledger.

"Did I miss the joke?" he asked, returning her smile.

"Hardly," Jenny answered. "There's no way you're going to miss this one."

Daniel stared at her for a moment before realizing what Jenny was getting at. "Are you having contractions?"

Jenny nodded. "About every five minutes. They started about breakfast time."

Daniel looked at his watch. "That's been little less than an hour, and already they're coming every five minutes?"

Jenny opened her mouth to reply, but pain ripped through her and she doubled over instead. Daniel was at her side in a flash, calling for Lillie and helping Jenny to a bed.

"Make that every three minutes," Jenny said as the pain eased.

Lillie came into the room chiding Daniel for yelling until she caught sight of Jenny on the bed. She immediately went to prepare the things Daniel would need for the delivery.

"Should I send for Garrett and David?" she asked as she went to put a pot of water on the stove.

"Send John for them. I don't think we have enough time to spare you," Daniel answered. Jenny was already grimacing through another contraction.

Lillie nodded and added, "I'll get her into a nightgown as soon as I send John."

Suddenly, Jenny screamed, and Lillie ran in search of her son.

Daniel came to Jenny's side and removed her shoes. "Oh, Daniel," Jenny said as she gripped his arm. "I feel like I'm being torn apart inside."

"Just try to relax," Daniel advised, knowing how ridiculous it was to suggest such a thing. "I've sent John for David, and —"

"No," Jenny interrupted. "Don't let him be here. I can't bear for him to suffer again."

"Jenny, David has a right to be here. He wouldn't want it any other way, and he'd have my hide if I refused to let him be at your side," Daniel said as Lillie entered the room with Jenny's bedclothes.

"I don't, I . . ." Jenny's words faded into a cry which she muffled as she bit into the back of her hand. "I thought I'd have more time. The pains are so much worse. I think the baby is coming now!"

Daniel checked her condition and nodded to Lillie. "We don't have time to change her, Lillie. She's going to deliver any minute. Did you send John?"

"Yes," Lillie answered and wiped a cool cloth across Jenny's forehead. "They should be here any minute."

"Ask them to wait in the sitting room," Daniel said and saw gratitude flicker in Jenny's eyes. Lillie's face questioned her husband's words, but she went outside to wait for David and Garrett.

In less than a minute, David and Garrett came on the run with little John held securely in Garrett's sturdy arms. Lillie met them on the walk. "Daniel wants you to wait in the sitting room," she said as she pulled David along with her.

"No, I want to see Jenny. I want to be with her," David protested. "Something's wrong, isn't it?"

"No," Lillie said gently. "Daniel seldom allows the father to attend the actual birth. You'll be within earshot, though. You'll hear everything from Daniel chewing me out for handing him the wrong instrument, to your baby's first cry," she added lightheartedly.

"But, I was there for her before, and I

want to be there for her this time," David argued.

"Maybe it would make it easier for Jenny if we waited in the other room," Garrett said as he put John down. "In fact, it would probably be very helpful to Lillie and Daniel if we were keeping an eye on the boys for them."

"Yes, it would," Lillie added before David could offer further protest.

"You'd best go help Daniel. I'll keep an eye on David," Garrett said as he opened the door and ushered David into the sitting room. Lillie nodded and went to retrieve the water from the stove.

"John, you mind your Uncle David and Garrett. I'll be helping Aunt Jenny and Papa, so you be a good boy and play nicely with James."

"I will, Mama," John said as he went to his room in search of his brother.

Lillie came back through the room with a kettle of hot water just as Jenny let out a scream. David would have jumped to his feet, but Garrett held him back.

"I'd best get in there," Lillie said with no other explanation.

Daniel was working feverishly with Jenny when Lillie came in with the water. "I was beginning to wonder if you'd deserted me,"

Daniel said as Lillie poured water into the basin.

"David and Garrett are watching the boys in the sitting room," Lillie explained and stopped dead in her tracks as Daniel delivered Jenny's baby. The baby's hearty cry filled the air.

"It's a boy," Lillie said excitedly as she wiped Jenny's brow. "Oh Jenny, he's beautiful."

"You'd better take him," Daniel said suddenly. "Something's not quite right."

His serious tone caused Lillie to drop her cloth immediately. The baby continued to cry and he looked healthy to Lillie, but Jenny was still in pain.

Daniel was intent on his work, and Lillie found it impossible to read his expression. Was Jenny dying? Lillie tried to ignore her fears and wrapped the baby in a blanket. Daniel's laughter in contrast to Jenny's cry caused Lillie to nearly drop the infant.

"What in the world are you laughing about?" Lillie asked as she hugged the crying baby close.

"This," Daniel said as he delivered a second crying baby. "Mrs. Monroe, you have twins."

Jenny joined Daniel's laughter. Lillie caught the joy of the moment. "Twins! And this one is a girl! Oh, Jenny, congratulations!"

David came bursting through the doorway with a stunned expression on his face. "Did I hear you right? Did Jenny really have twins?"

Garrett was right behind him with an apologetic look on his face.

"She certainly did!" Lillie exclaimed. "You have a son and a daughter."

Jenny wiped tears of joy from her eyes. "God is truly amazing," she whispered as she took her son from Lillie's arms.

David came to Jenny's side, while Garrett ushered John and James back into the sitting room. "Is she . . . I mean . . ." David awkwardly searched for words to ask about Jenny's condition.

Daniel read his brother's thoughts. "Jenny is fine, David. She's in good shape, and from the sound of it, so are the babies."

Jenny handed her son to David and accepted her newly wrapped daughter from Lillie. "Oh, David. They're beautiful."

David nodded and wiped a tear from his eye. "So are you, Jenny."

"Any regrets?" Jenny asked as she pulled back the covers to better see her son.

"No," David said with a grin. "You?"

"Not one. Like Hannah in the Bible I

asked for a child, but God gave me two. I'm truly a blessed woman."

"What are you going to name them?" Lillie asked.

Jenny looked at David and smiled.

"I think Hannah would be appropriate for our daughter," David said as he reached over to touch the baby's fine, brown hair.

Jenny nodded. "I'd like that," she said, then reached up to touch her son's cheek. " 'She bare a son, and called his name Samuel,' " she quoted 1 Samuel 1:20, " 'saying, Because I have asked him of the Lord.' "

"Hannah and Samuel," Lillie declared. "I think those names are most fitting."

"And I think it would be most fitting to allow this new family a bit of time alone," Daniel said, pulling Lillie toward the door. "I'll be back to check up on you in a little while."

Jenny and David nodded but said nothing as they continued to study their babies.

"I can't say I'm not afraid," David finally spoke. "I mean, seeing them like this is almost more frightening. Now I have the future to worry about."

"No," Jenny said as she placed her hand upon her husband's arm. "The future belongs to the Lord."

"But everything is different now," David

said and looked deep into Jenny's brown eyes. "So many things have come to an end: our home, the work with the Indians. So much has changed."

"But change isn't necessarily bad," Jenny chided. "Change brought us Hannah and Samuel. Change gave us a new ministry here in Bandelero."

"Do you think Garrett was right? Has God led us in a new direction? Are we to abandon our mission with the Indians and minister to this town instead? And what about the children? I can't bear the thought of losing them to death."

"Death is a powerful force," Jenny agreed as she nestled Hannah against her breast, "but then, so is love."

David thought for a moment, taking in the sight of his wife and children. The joy he felt was like none he'd ever known. " 'Set me as a seal upon thine heart,' " he quoted, remembering Song of Solomon 8:6. " 'As a seal upon thine arm: for love is strong as death.' " David smiled. "You're right, Jen."

"I pledge you my love, now and forever," Jenny said as she lifted her face to David's. "It doesn't matter where the journey takes us, it only matters that I make it with you."

David cupped Jenny's face in his free hand

and pressed his lips to hers. Wherever God led them, no matter the distance, no matter the cost, they journeyed with God. His love had already proven stronger than death.

ABOUT THE AUTHOR

Tracie Peterson, best-selling author of over forty fiction titles and one nonfiction title, lives and works in Topeka, Kansas. As a Christian, wife, mother, and writer (in that order), Tracie finds her slate quite full.

First published as a columnist for the *Kansas Christian* newspaper, Tracie resigned that position to turn her attention to novels. After signing her first contract with Barbour Publishing in 1992, her first novel appeared in 1993 under the pen name of Janelle Jamison, and the rest is history. She has over twenty-three titles with Heartsong Presents' book club and stories in six separate anthologies from Barbour, including the best-selling *Alaska.* From Bethany House Publishing, Tracie has several historical series, as well as a variety of women's fiction titles.

Voted favorite author for 1995, 1996, and 1997 by the Heartsong Presents readership, Tracie enjoys the pleasure of spinning stories for readers and thanks God for the imagination He's given. "I find myself blessed to be able to work at a job I love. I get to travel, study history, spin yarns, spend time with my family, and hopefully glorify God. I can't imagine a more perfect arrangement."

Tracie also does acquisitions work for Barbour Publishing and teaches workshops at a variety of conferences, giving workshops on inspirational romance, historical research, and anything else that offers assistance to fellow writers.

See Tracie on the Internet at http://members.aol.com/tjpbooks/.

EC